Hungary-Hollywood Express

When Gabriel Rivages recounts the life of Olympic gold medalist and silver-screen heart-throb Johnny Weissmuller (1904-1984), he brings to life a vibrant patchwork of America's 20th century, from its athletic exploits to its literary underground, from its cinematic glory to its obscure failures. Burroughs sells pencil sharpeners, Einstein crosses paths with squirrel hunters, JFK becomes an airport, the world record for the 100-metre freestyle swim is broken, Tarzan saves Jane, a corrupt accountant runs away with the savings, World War II makes waves in Lake Michigan, and a living legend wraps up a storied career as a host in a Las Vegas restaurant.

Hungary-Hollywood Express is the first novel in Éric Plamondon's *1984* trilogy. The second and third volumes, *Mayonnaise* and *Apple S*, turn their lens on the poet Richard Brautigan and Apple founder Steve Jobs respectively, and will also be published by Esplanade Books, translated by Dimitri Nasrallah.

"A novel for the Wikipedia generation."
–Dominque Tardif, *Voir Magazine*

ÉRIC PLAMONDON was born in Québec in 1969 and currently lives in Bordeaux. When his *1984* trilogy was first published it was quickly considered a shining example of a new generation of Québécois literary innovation. All three books have recently been published in one volume.

DIMITRI ASRALLAH, the author of two award-winning novels. *Niko* won the Hugh MacLennan Fiction Prize & was longlisted for the International IMPAC Dublin Award.

ISBN: 978-1-55065-450-9 $19.95
Trade paper | French flaps | 5x7½ | 160 pp

PUBLICITY
Maya Assouad | 514.844.6073 |
marketing@vehiculepress

VOLUME 1 OF THE 1984 TRILOGY

Hungary-Hollywood Express

A NOVEL

ÉRIC PLAMONDON

TRANSLATED FROM THE FRENCH BY
DIMITRI NASRALLAH

ESPLANADE
Books

THE FICTION SERIES AT VÉHICULE PRESS

Published with the generous assistance of the Canada Council for the Arts, the Canada Book Fund of the Department of Canadian Heritage, and the Société de développement des entreprises culturelles du Québec (SODEC). We acknowledge the financial support of the Government of Canada through the National Translation Program for Book Publishing, an initiative of the *Roadmap for Canada's Official Languages 2013-2018: Education, Immigration, Communities*, for our translation activities.

Esplanade Books editor : Dimitri Nasrallah
Cover design: David Drummond
Photo of author: Rodolphe Escher/Le Quartanier
Typeset in Minion by Simon Garamond
Printed by Marquis Printing Inc.

Originally published as *Hongrie-Hollywood Express*
by Le Quartanier, 2011.

Published by Véhicule Press, Montréal, Québec, Canada
vehiculepress.com

Printed in Canada on FSC® certified paper.

Simplicity is the ultimate sophistication.
STEVE JOBS

Seldom have I known any profound being that had
anything to say to this world, unless forced to stammer
out something by way of getting a living.
HERMAN MELVILLE

CONTENTS

1.

LAST CHANCE

I'm about to turn forty and the questions that I asked myself at twenty are still burning, undecided, unresolved. I've had acne, I went to university, I fucked around, I got married, I took drugs, I travelled, I played sports, I read newspapers, I said "hello", I said "yes, thank you", I was class president, I was employee of the month, I fought for this cause and I fought for that cause. I opened a bank account, I saved, I bought a car, I drove a little drunk but not a lot, I didn't burn through red lights, I ironed my shirts on Sunday evenings, I bought gifts for Christmas, birthdays, weddings, Valentine's Day. I've taken out life insurance, I bought a flat screen, a laptop, I've recycled empty bottles, paper, cardboard, plastic. I've eaten fruits and vegetables and dairy products. I've turned off lights when leaving, I made sure faucets were closed tightly, I washed my hands, and I never pissed on the toilet seat. I traded in my vinyl records for cassettes, then my cassettes for CDs and my CDs for mp3s. I've got leather shoes for work, Reeboks for sport, cleats for the mountain, and galoshes for the rain.

I watched Orson Welles' *Citizen Kane* because it's the biggest film in cinematic history. I watched *Titanic* because it's the film that was watched by the largest number of viewers in cinematic history. I watched *The Seven Year Itch* because it contains cinematic history's most iconic scene, in which Marilyn holds down her white dress atop the subway grates. I watched *Pierrot le Fou* because the New Wave changed cinematic history. I watched *Jaws* because my father wanted to take me to the movies. I watched *Star Wars* because I was ten. I read *Brave New World* because it was on the curriculum. I read Agatha Christie's *Ten Little Indians* and Ernest Callenbach's *Ecotopia* for the same reason. I've played baseball, I've played handball, I've played volleyball, I've played football, I've played badminton but I never played hockey. At fourteen, I picked vegetables to learn what it was to work. At fifteen, I worked as a babysitter to pay for the movies, a pair of jeans, a pack of beer, and an Iron Maiden album. At sixteen, I pumped gas so I could spend a week camping in Cape Cod. At seventeen, I worked as a librarian to pay the return bus fare between Quebec City and Thetford Mines. At eighteen, I worked as a host at the Educative Society of Canada to pay for a shared apartment, and I worked as a waiter to eat.

I've owned a tricycle, I've owned roller skates, ice skates, a skateboard, a 10-speed Gitane, a moped, a Honda Civic, a Renault 5, a Ford Horizon, a Peugeot 305, a Peugeot 306, and a Peugeot 307.

I developed an allergy to cat hair, I smoked a pack a day for ten years and then I stopped. I kept my wisdom teeth, I donated my sperm. I shattered a bus shelter. I built a house.

I've been a model, a journalist, a waiter, a farmhand. I've worked at a cement plant, in a hardware store, and in a chemistry lab. I've been a French instructor and an English instructor. I've done theatre and I've pumped gas at a Petro-Canada managed by Ti-Cul Perron.

I've fished trout from the banks of rivers. I've fished bass from canoes on lakes. I've fished gudgeon from streams, I've fished salmon with a fly.

I've listened to disco, rock, heavy metal, jazz, fusion, prog, country, grunge, classical, baroque, opera, and world music.

I've smoked weed and hash, I've snorted coke and mesc, I've swallowed acid and ecstasy. I've gotten pissed from beer, I've gotten pissed from whisky, I've gotten pissed from red wine, I've gotten pissed from rum and from vodka. I've mixed, I've vomited, I've woken up with hangovers and done it all again, numerous times.

I've read Diderot, I've read Voltaire, I've read the Bible. I've read Shakespeare, I've read Melville, I've read Rabelais. I've read Baudelaire, I've read Flaubert, I've read Ducharme. I've read Pynchon, Williams, Capote, Irving and above all Brautigan. I've read Kerouac. I've read Miller, I've read Rimbaud, I've read Camus. And then also Blanchot, Yourcenar, Sartre, Bakhtin, Céline, Cyrano, Hesse, McLuhan, Sterne, Zola. I've also flipped through Plato, Nietzsche, Barthes, Freud, Newton, and Galileo.

I've been cross-country skiing, alpine skiing, snow-shoeing, rowboating, windsurfing, and scuba-diving. I've surfed, skydived, and wiped out in motocross. I've done tobogganing, rafting, and a little bit of spelunking.

I've caught toads, frogs, garter snakes, tadpoles, grasshoppers, snails, butterflies, caterpillars, mice, and voles. I've trapped marmots, muskrats, squirrels, and foxes. I've hunted partridge and set up rabbit snares.

I've ridden a Ski-doo, I've ridden a Sea-doo, I've watched *Scooby-Doo*. I've watched *Dallas*, *The Incredible Hulk*, *The Dukes of Hazard*, and *Knight Rider*. On Saturday nights, back when I was young, I had dinner in front of *Space: 1999*. For four years on December 31st, Michel Fugain & Le Big Bazar struck in my New Year's Eve. While I played with my Lego on Saturday mornings, *Candy Candy*, *Belle and Sebastian*, *Captain Future*, and *Captain Harlock* flickered on the screen.

One summer, my dad took me to Old Orchard Beach in Maine. After three days of camping in the rain, we came back. Later, my mom took me to Ogunquit, which went better. The following year, it was Toronto and Niagara Falls. I participated in a student exchange program to Calgary.

When I was five years old, I visited Montreal, Rome, Amsterdam, Seville, Munich, Venice, Bordeaux, Paris, Bruges, and Auschwitz. When I was twenty-three years old I did it all again, going from Paris to Nice, then Monaco, then Brindisi, then Athens, then Corfu, then Rome, Geneva, Luxembourg, Bruges, Amsterdam, and back to Paris before returning to Quebec City.

I studied the sciences and mathematics (integral and differential calculus), and I took courses in politics (totalitarianism according to Hannah Arendt) and economics (Adam Smith's invisible hand and Schumpeter's creative destruction). I also studied the history of cinema (from *Battleship Potemkin* to Frank Capra) and the historical novel (from Racine to Yourcenar).

I've traveled charter, I've traveled economy class, I've traveled business class, and I've traveled first class. I've crossed Canada by bus, I've crossed Europe by train. I've crossed the Atlantic in a 747, a 737, a DC-10 and an A-320.

I've participated on reading committees and editorial committees, I've sat with the board of directors, I've done brainstorming sessions, weekly reviews, monthly meetings. I've been project leader, coordinator, assistant, manager, director, and president. I've written summaries, technical manuals, I've implemented strategies.

I've made love in the snow, I've made love in a pool, I've made love on a plane. I've fucked in the kitchen, I've fucked in the living room, in the den. I've fucked on a washing machine, I've fucked in a stairwell, I've fucked in a car, I've fucked in the middle of a field, under a tree, in the shower, and in a castle tower.

I've eaten poutine in Trois-Rivières, I've dined on goulash in Budapest, I've eaten schnitzels in Prague, I've eaten tapas in Seville. I've eaten a pizza in Naples, duck confit in Bordeaux, steak frites in Paris, grilled chicken in Porto, sausage in Strasbourg, lobster in Saly Portudal, suckling pig in Hong Kong, fajitas in Hollywood, pad thai in Toronto, and a burger in New York.

I've given crayons to kids living in the baobab forests of Senegal. I've bought drugs by taxi in a Chicago ghetto.

I've snorted coke in a Montreal tavern. I've eaten at Gaudí's Casa Batlló in Barcelona. I've pissed in the toilets of the Peninsula in Kowloon. I had my bags searched at the Ritz-Carlton in Istanbul. I've served beers to Renaud around the time he was singing "Miss Maggie". I've traveled next to Luc Plamondon as he slept. I've won story contests, photo contests. I've won a bronze medal, a silver medal, and a gold medal. I've lost many races.

I've repaired a washing machine, I've repaired a vacuum cleaner, I've done plumbing, I've put up a wall, I've assembled a chicken coop, a doghouse, a table, a couch, and a birdhouse.

I've dissected dead bodies, I've filmed surgeries. I've dined with directors and surgeons, accountants, secretaries and economists, architects and the unemployed, professors and mechanics, the big, the fat, the small, the weak.

I've owned a Texas Instrument 99/4A, I've owned a Commodore VIC-20, I've owned a Macintosh Classic, a Power Mac, a G3, a G4, a G5. I've learned how to use Windows, Outlook, Word, Excel, Photoshop, Dreamweaver, Flash, Final Cut, Motion, Netscape, Gopher, iTunes, Quark-XPress, PageMaker, InDesign, Toast, and After Effects.

I've done layout, brochures, posters, books, video editing, digital shooting, 3D animation, audio mixing, photography. I signed myself up for Facebook, I created a blog, I used Google Docs, I opened a Yahoo account, a Free account, a Hotmail account.

I've also been a soldier. I've cut off cocks, heads, and arms. I've raped young girls and run over women with

18

a Hummer. I've blown up embassies, I've gone AWOL. I saved lives, bandaged wounds, and fed children.

I've seen the Twin Towers on fire. I've seen a journalist beheaded like Saint John the Baptist. I've seen Salome belly dance. I've seen Genghis Khan's elephants cross the Mongol Empire, I've seen Roland carve the Pyrenees with his sword. I've seen Mount Vesuvius destroy Pompeii and Erina, who screamed as lava melted her feet, her legs, her trunk, her head, linger in her last look at me. I've seen Geronimo charge a cavalry line. I've seen skulls scalped by Iroquois. I've seen skulls scalped by white men. Under the watchful eye of Moctezuma, I took part in the sacrifice of six thousand virgins. I stabbed Caesar, I took the streetcar with Brando. I've leapt from the top of the Statue of Liberty. I've pissed blood under the blade of Guillotin's invention. I've been shot in the neck and seen my blood splatter across the floor. I've seen the firing line before being blindfolded. I've soldered the bodies of Fords in Detroit. I sold everything in '29 before turning on the gas. I've died in the electric chair, and I've worked at Menlo Park.

In Vietnam I burned children alive with napalm. I climbed the stage at Woodstock. I set a foot on the moon. I fired at Kennedy. I bombed London. I entered Havana with Castro. I carried the stones for the Great Wall of China. I led a revolution with Mao. I was a Bolshevik. I blessed the Assembly. I've harpooned whales. I've sold brushes. I inaugurated the Panama Canal.

I've marched against nuclear energy, against the death penalty, against low wages, against the church, against violence, against war, against colonialism, against the cult of personality, against the massacre of Indians, against circumcision, and I've filmed orgies in the Californian villas of Malibu.

And now, I'm going to swim the 100-meter freestyle in under a minute.

2

JÀNOS

Johnny Weissmuller, born Jànos, entered the world in a little village of the Austro-Hungarian Empire at the start of the twentieth century. More precisely, he was born on June 2nd, 1904, in Szabadfalu, and he would come to embody, in immaculate perfection, the last of the great myths: Tarzan, the Ape Man.

3

VERSO

Gabriel Rivages was conceived in May 1968 in the back-woods of a Canadian forest. In Paris, they called it the unrestrained pursuit of pleasure. His mother, a waitress at the only hotel on a wildlife reserve, had succumbed to the charms of a foreman. Gabriel was born on February 13, 1969, the same day the Quebec Liberation Front detonated a bomb at the Montreal Stock Exchange. The president of the exchange noted the event with irony: "Today, you might say that the market went up!"

At the age of forty, Gabriel Rivages feared his life hadn't amounted to much. After the women, the drugs, the travels, the books, the many jobs, and the children, he still felt a deep-seated emptiness inside him. He fills it with everything he can get his hands on.

4

BIBLIOGRAPHICAL REFERENCES

Title: *Tarzan of the Apes*

Author: Edgar Rice Burroughs

First release date: August 1, 1993 [eBook #78]

Language: English

Character set encoding: ASCII

START OF THIS PROJECT GUTENBERG EBOOK
TARZAN OF THE APES

Produced by Judith Boss. HTML version by Al Haines.

CONTENTS

5

IT SMELLS OF FIR

Gabriel Rivages was born on February 13, 1969, at 8:50 pm. It was snowing all across Quebec City. During the final contractions, his mother wavered between the imminent birth and thoughts of suicide. The violent convulsions within her abdomen only made her want to vomit. She buckled, unable to suffer more pain. Since her room was on the fifth floor, during the lulls she said to herself, if only I could get myself up, break the glass, and jump.

> It smells of fir,
> rain was coming
> under the stars of the day.
> She looked over my seven years.
> She didn't dare,
> so I asked her,
> I wanted to know why,
> why I felt like crying.
> She said, "I'm leaving now"
> and so I cried.

6

MOLITOR

In 1929, near one of Paris's largest public gardens, the Bois de Boulogne, the Molitor pool opened with a lavish inauguration presided over by Johnny Weissmuller and Aileen Riggin, an Olympic diving champion. At twenty-five years old, and three years prior to his role as Tarzan in the movies, Weissmuller was known around the world for his five Olympic gold medals. A lifeguard in his spare time, he worked at the Molitor during the summer of 1929. The pool also hosted fashion shows, theatrical performances, and training sessions for figure skaters.

I'm particularly fond of the photo where we see Weiss-muller and Riggin, water up to their waists, in Molitor bathing suits. They're standing side by side, and he looks a little apprehensive. It's almost as if, there, in the water, they want to get closer to each other, maybe even em-brace, but they won't dare, frozen before the lens. In 1929, the two champions were far from the stock-market crash, far from America, far from home. The more I look at the photo, the more I see something between them. I see them going back to the hotel, having a drink at the bar, and sharing a good laugh at the funny accents of all the French around them. A little later, they climb the red-carpeted steps of the hotel's grand staircase together.

Caption: *"Aileen Riggin, campeã olimpica americana de saltos ornamentais. E Johnnny Weissmuller, o Tarzan, nas Piscinas Molitor (1929)."*

7

SZABADFALU

It's hot. It's June 24, 1941. We're in Freidorf, Romania. We're in a war. In 1904, this same village was called Szabadfalu. It was part of the Austro-Hungarian Empire. Today, two soldiers from the Third Reich are at the mayor's office. They're scouring the registers. The mayor helps them. They're hunting for deserters. All men old enough to fight must join the troops. We're in a war.

Near four o'clock, one of the soldiers finds a discrepancy. Someone named Jànos Weiszmueller is missing from the call. The mayor is questioned. He knows exactly where to find him – at the village cinema.

Fifteen minutes later, the two soldiers burst into the dark theatre. They order the house lights on. The bigger of the two bellows, "Where's the citizen named Jànos Weiszmueller hiding?" In seemingly the same motion, the entire audience turns and points to the screen. There he is, Johnny Weissmuller, in his first film for Metro-Goldwyn-Mayer: *Tarzan the Ape Man*.

8

EVOLUTION

Seems that the Earth turns—on itself and around the Sun. Mm-hmm. There have been people burned alive for saying as much. Seems also that the universe is expanding, that the Sun will burn out in a couple billion years and that, in the beginning, man was nothing more than a tiny bit of seaweed. They say that the ozone layer has been punctured and that in less than a century there won't be any more drinkable water left. And that margarine and cellphones can lead to cancer.

As for me, yesterday I read a book: *Tokyo-Montana Express*. The guy who wrote it was named Richard Brautigan. I say *was named* because in 1984 he was found dead in his California home, a revolver at his side.

9

THIRD CLASS

Elizabeth and Petrus board the *S.S. Rotterdam* on January 14, 1905. They're going to cross the Atlantic in the dead of winter. The *S.S. Rotterdam* sets off from the city of the same name to New York. For twelve days, Elizabeth and Petrus live in the ship's bilge. They're third-class passengers. They sleep in the deepest part of the ship, beneath the waterline. Because they are poor, and you really have to be poor to spend twelve days in the belly of the beast. In the deep and dark dormitory where rats roam, they cough, spit, shit in buckets, scratch themselves, bitch, bawl, and above all, above everything, in the middle of the ocean, they vomit. Elizabeth carries, in her arms, her seven-month-old son. America truly possesses a glamorous and powerful attraction.

10

EINSTEIN

In 1905, Johnny nurses his mother's breast and Einstein asks the following question: "Does the inertia of a body depend upon its energy-content?" Johnny's father found a job at a coalmine in Windber, Pennsylvania. Einstein answers: "$E=mc^2$."

POISSON

Thursday, 2:30 pm, I'm in my Probabilities and Statistics for Economists course. The prof lectures and I take notes:

"In probability theory and in statistics, the Poisson distribution is a discrete probability distribution that describes the likelihood of a given number of events being produced in a fixed interval of time, if these events occur…"

At five, I go by my apartment to get ready. I change out of my jeans and t-shirt and into pleated black slacks and a presentable white button-down shirt. I have a change pouch containing a hundred dollars, my apron, my corkscrew, my notebook, and my pen.

Thirty minutes later, I've arrived at the restaurant. I've looked over the schedule. I've been assigned evening service in Section C. I've checked the set up: the glasses for water, the wine carafes, the garbage bags, the cutlery, the coffee cups, and the tea bags. I've gone into the kitchen to ask what's on the table d'hôte: on the menu, fish. My first two customers arrived around 6 pm. They didn't want an aperitif. He ordered the table d'hôte, she went with the pasta. I entered my code in the computer, I tapped in 107 for the table number, 2 for the number of people and 0 for "Beverages". When I returned with the bread, they'd decided to take a half-bottle of Entre-Deux-Mers. Two businessmen sat down at 102. I passed by and said good evening. I returned to the computer, my code, 107, beverages: ½ Entre-Deux-Mers, I pressed "Order". I came back around to 102 and asked if they might like aperitifs: a Laurentide and a Bloody Mary. Three people at 105, a teenager with her parents. 107's entrée was ready in the kitchen. I served the salad with a 'bon appétit'. The two businessmen were ready to order. I said good evening to 105 and checked that the hostess had indeed set them up with menus. A Caesar salad and a steak frites, which I noted in my notebook. At the bar, the Laurentide, the Bloody Mary, and the half-bottle of white awaited me. A colleague asked me if I wouldn't mind changing a ten for two fives. I tapped in 105's order on the computer. I got going on the next course for 107. I took plates back to the dishwashers. I had a moment of concern for the two guys who were still waiting. I brought them bread, I took another order, I'd forgotten glasses of water, I came back to see if anything was ready, a quarter of red at the bar. I gave Maryse a helping hand in serving the next course to the table with the girl dressed in red. I still had several free tables in my section. An older gentleman with a news-paper sat down in 103.

The peak hour arrived. There were customers to greet, to seat, to set up with menus, to bring water, to ack-nowledge with hellos, remove entrée plates for 4 then prepare a coffee and a tea for 32, settle up the little couple in blue, collect the last tip, take back the daily special to the kitchen for 14, they're pressed for time, they have a rendezvous anywhere, somewhere, a funeral for all I know, finally then, we have to set up 105 for one person. Don't forget to tell them that there's no more soup with the daily special, cut the bread, prepare three pitchers of water. Someone has to go down to the cellar, draft number three is empty. The banker at 3 knocked over his glass of red.

That was Thursday evening. Thursday evenings are big nights. There were eight of us on the floor. For three hours, we worked non-stop. We were in over our heads for a little while, but not by much. Once the rush passed, my legs were sore, I finished clearing my tables, I emptied my garbage can, I had a shirttail sticking out from my pants, my apron was stained. We sat down at the table reserved for the wait-staff and each tallied our takings. The moment of truth: on a ticket appeared the total amount of your sales for the night. In your pouch, a big roll of bills, all the receipts, including your tips and the petty cash. We pay the house, we deduct our cut and, if the night was excellent, we find ourselves with eighty extra dollars, our tips. That's pretty much how we do it. Once everything's closed up, we head to the bar to drink.

Tina served me a Bud. It was already getting close to last call. So she could finish up sooner, I helped her restock the beer fridge. She wiped everything down, the lights were all turned on. Two customers remained in the back, bags under their eyes. We gathered our things, tired, but we still had some adrenaline remaining in our empty stomachs. We went dancing. By four in the morning, my tips had evaporated. Statistically, it was quite unlikely that I would have a career in the restaurant business or in economics. Poisson was onto something.

12

EMMA LAZARUS

The *S.S. Rotterdam* has passed before Liberty Enlightening the World. The poem engraved on her pedestal is too far. Millions of immigrants have passed before it, but how many have read the words by Emma Lazarus?

Give me your tired, your poor,
Your huddled masses yearning to breathe free,
The wretched refuse of your teeming shore,
Send these, the homeless, tempest-tost to me,
I lift my lamp beside the golden door!

—*The New Colossus*, 1883

13

LATE

The Statue of Liberty was inaugurated on October 28, 1886, by Grover Cleveland, the only American president to serve two nonconsecutive terms in the White House. As an honour to the young republic that proclaimed rights and liberties to equality and happiness, France offered the United States of America a copper statue thirty-seven meters tall. Imagined by Frédéric Auguste Bartholdi and constructed by Gustave Eiffel, Liberty Enlightening the World is, today, the most visited monument in the United States.

France wanted to offer the Statue of Liberty to America as a celebration of the one-hundredth anniversary of the Declaration of Independence. The statue was supposed to be delivered in 1876. France was ten years late.

14

ELECTRIC ERECTION

She stood there,
before me,
like a wire
stripped.

15

REVENGE

In 1867, Bartholdi visits the Egyptian viceroy, Khedive Isma'il Pasha. He has a lighthouse project for the Suez Canal, which Lesseps is in the midst of digging. He draws, makes sketch after sketch, writes, sets up meetings, discusses, then obtains an appointment with the khedive.

It's 11 am. It's already very hot on Cairo's streets. With his rolls under his arms, Bartholdi climbs the palace steps. He waits in an antechamber.

After a very long wait, he finds himself before two grand, golden doors. The viceroy receives him. Across a large mahogany table, he unrolls his drafts. A beautiful woman draped in long robes spreads across the table. A torch in hand, she rests upon a giant granite pedestal. She's Egypt bringing light to Asia. This is the lighthouse that Bartholdi proposes to the khedive. A lighthouse made to measure for the Suez Canal.

The figure of the beautiful Egyptian imagined by Bartholdi was inspired directly from a famous painting by Delacroix: Liberty leading the People, a woman with breasts exposed standing atop the Parisian barricades.

But, with a simple shake of the head, the khedive rejects Bartholdi and his sketches of a woman-shaped lighthouse.

These days, more than two million people visit the Statue of Liberty each year. Bartholdi has been avenged.

16

PENCIL SHARPENER

This is the story of a poor guy who sold pencil sharpeners in Chicago, 1911. Things had started off relatively well for him. His father had money. He'd attended the Michigan Military Academy. He was supposed to go to West Point. But he fails the entrance exam. By and by, he finds himself in Arizona, in a cavalry regiment. One evening, after kilometers of trotting and galloping, he collapses. Medical exams reveal he has a heart problem. His military career ends there, in Arizona, one evening in July 1897.

He struggles for a brief time, working at several ranches in the area. His father offers him a job, but it isn't what he wants. What he wants is the city, the big city. That would be Chicago.

But his struggles continue. They continue to the point that he finds himself selling pencil sharpeners. The only advantage of the job is the free time. And during that free time, he reads. He devours pulp magazines. And the more he devours them, the more he finds them vacant. They pass the time, but frankly our pencil-sharpener salesman can't believe that people are paid to write stories this bad. He tells himself he could write them much better. So that's what he does. He sharpens many pencils and he's off.

One year later, he receives four hundred dollars for *Under the Moons of Mars*. A fortune in 1912. But all this is nothing compared to what the adventures of his next character will bring him: Tarzan, the ape man.

17

SGT. PEPPER

When I was young, my best friend was my cousin Luc. He was like my brother. I was eight years old and he was twelve. He was also my hero, in a way. For his birthday, he'd received the Beatles' red album. I can see us in the basement, the music blaring. We sang, "She loves you, yeah yeah yeah", without understanding any of it. So it was my cousin Luc who introduced me to the Beatles. Much later Paul McCartney sang "Say Say Say" with Michael Jackson. But that's another story.

My story with the Beatles is really the red album. They're all there, on the balcony, they're looking down. To make me happy, my dad bought me the blue album. But it was the red one that I wanted.

Today, what brings me back to the Beatles is another record, *Sgt. Pepper's Lonely Hearts Club Band*. It's superb. It was released June 1st, 1967. Moreover, behind Ringo, tucked in between Marilyn and Edgar Allan Poe, he's there, in black and white, his head jutting out: Johnny Weissmuller.

After the Beatles, my cousin Luc made me listen to Kiss, Styx, and Led Zeppelin. After that, we lost touch.

18

A.E.I.O.U.

Austria Est Imperare Orbi Universo. Austria's destiny is to rule the whole world. That was the Habsburg's slogan. Petrus was fed up with everything. Elizabeth had given birth seven months ago. On January 14, 1905, they leave Holland aboard the *S.S. Rotterdam*. They cross the Atlantic. It's winter. They are at the bottom of the hold: third-class passengers. Sleeping with the rats. No water. Suffocating, vomiting, gasping, and drifting toward America. If rats is all there is to eat, then rats it is. For America, everything is up for grabs. The baby's finally sleeping. It all begins in the belly of the beast.

ARMELLE AND GIONO

Now the Lord provided a huge fish to swallow Jonah, and Jonah was in the belly of the fish three days and three nights.

From this biblical passage, Melville in *Moby Dick* arrives at this:

"Delight is to him, who gives no quarter in the truth, and kills, burns, and destroys all sin though he pluck it from under the robes of Senators and Judges."

But that's how Giono translated the passage.

Armel Guerne translated it this way:

"Great delight to him who, for the truth, gives no quarter, who kills, burns, and destroys all sin, even in exposing and plucking it out from under the robes of Senators and the robes of Judges."

That reminds me of Armelle, who'd traveled from Paris to Montreal to study at UQAM. That's where I met her. She had skin as soft as Bible paper. I remember her breasts. They were a sight to behold, perfectly poised. Magnificent breasts, practically suspended in air. When I pulled back her dress, they looked like they were calling my hands, and the Lord saw that it was good.

20

A QUESTION OF PRINCIP

His mother gave him water wings. He'd turned ten at the beginning of the month. Today is Sunday. It's hot and humid. For once, the windy city is that only in name. Flags fly at half-mast. It's hot in Chicago. Two children walk toward the lake. They pass under the skytrain. It's early in the afternoon. It's a full-on heatwave. The swim that awaits will relieve them of all that, of the heat, of their alcoholic father, of their crying mother, of the beatings, of the city. When he dives, when he leaps, when he floats out, he doesn't even feel the water, he's not swimming but flying, he's gliding along the current. He and his brother can spend hours, days, like this. But going back is not a question, it's beginning to get late, and we're dying of hunger. We'll nevertheless dive in one more time, one more walk across the wharf. He gets up, climbs, all the way to the top. It always makes his stomach tingle a little to see the lake from that high up. And he jumps, he falls, and he gains momentum, and his naked skin explodes into the water. We hear an enormous detonation, it's June 28, 1914. Gavrilo Princip

47

has just fired at the Archduke Franz Ferdinand. Johnny breaks out in laughter. He was scared, but it didn't hurt. Seven thousand kilometers from here, the First World War is about to break out.

21

AL

1931, Johnny marries Bobbe Arnst. He travels to Miami on a promotional tour for BVD swimsuits. Between swimming and diving showcases, he's at the hotel pool. He notices a solitary kid, head slumped in his shoulders. So during his break, Johnny, the kind man that he is, spends time with him and ends up teaching him how to swim. Then, one morning, no more kid, he's left just as inexplicably as he first appeared.

A few weeks later, Johnny receives a package at the hotel. It contains a magnificent gold watch. On the accompanying note, the following is written:

"Thanks for taking an interest in my son."

Signed: Al Capone.

22

AMERICA WITH A CAPITAL A

He is born on June 2, 1904, in a lost village of the Austro-Hungarian Empire. His father, Peter, is a retired captain in the army of Emperor Franz Joseph. His mother, Elizabeth, comes from a family of farmers that owns several chickens and a pig. They marry in 1904. In 1905, they pack their bags for America, America with a capital A.

23

RABELAIS

I left Quebec City to come here and join Annie-Anne, because in bed together we didn't sleep much. I decided to rebuild my life here. We got married so I could stay and because, in bed, we read Rabelais.

24

BACHRACH

One day in 1920, Jànos is introduced to the national swimming coach Ed Bachrach, who asks him to swim a few lengths. And then Bachrach watches in disbelief. This sixteen-year-old kid in the pool is kicking his feet at full speed. He has horrible technique, looks like he's drowning while advancing, cutting through the chlorinated water with his nose pointing up at the clock. His pace stuns Ed. He swims with his head up way too high, he displays no synchronicity, he breathes badly. But, as the legendary Ed himself would say a few years later when he spoke of that miraculous day: "A stopwatch never lies!"

It's been said that Weissmuller had developed this technique of the head above water on account of Lake Michigan. It was, for all intents, in that dirty water that he learned to swim. To avoid swallowing the floating filth, he swam with his head out of the water. This technique not only served him in winning gold medals, it also made him an excellent Tarzan. Van Dyke, the director, was overjoyed to be able to film close-ups of his face out of the water as he swam.

It's also been said that, for the role of Tarzan, Van Dyke (nicknamed "One-Take Woody") wanted an actor who could wear a loincloth without walking around like he was naked. Weissmuller had spent the first part of his life in a bathing suit before thousands of spectators. He was perfect. He was more at ease with a vine leaf across his hips than with a trench coat à la Bogart.

25

PAPER-LESS

Johnny won every competition in which he swam. He travels to Paris for the 1924 Olympic games. But he doesn't have papers certifying his American citizenship. Johnny Weissmuller was born in a country that no longer exists, in a town once called Szabadfalu that is now called Freidorf. His mother tells anyone who will listen that her son is a good American, the rumor spreads, it becomes a national matter. Will the great Olympic hope from Chicago be allowed to participate in the competition or not? He was born on June 2, 1904, in what is today the suburb of Timisoara.

It bears mentioning that we can't discount the determination of certain people.

Peter Junior, Johnny's brother, was born in Windber, Pennsylvania, in 1905. Let's modify the city register a touch, and there, the games are on. Someone added a little "Johnny" between Peter and Weissmuller. As a result, Peter Johnny Weissmuller was born in Windber in 1905, and his brother Peter Junior in 1904 in Freidorf. The old grow younger, and vice-versa.

Upon his return from France, the mayor of New York gave Johnny the key to the city. At the head of the athletes' parade, he came down 5th Avenue under confetti and cheering crowds.

26

HAIRS

In 1926, the four-time medal winner from the Paris Olympics is invited to visit the MGM studios in Hollywood. In near paralysis, he meets his childhood hero Douglas Fairbanks. The veteran actor gives him this advice: "If you ever do movies, make sure you shave your whole body, or else your hairs will appear huge onscreen. We won't be able to notice anything else. It's repulsive."

DEPARTMENT MEETING

I draw a square in the left-hand corner of the paper. I add some strokes. I make a cube. I make another cube. I connect the two cubes with four lines. I blacken one of the cubes. I add four circles. In one of the circles I add sunbeams. And underneath it I draw a triangle, then another. I draw a line. I crosshatch it. I divide the right corner of the paper into squares. I fill in every other square. The department meeting has already dragged on for forty-five minutes.

She's going to draw this meeting out beyond the hour it was expected to last. We review the projects for the month. We get stuck on the three days of training scheduled for next week. Three colleagues are talking at the same time. The room temperature holds at 20° c. The projector's ventilator is making a low hum. Beyond the window, I see the highway. Trucks and cars thread their way through grey dividers. On the side of the building across from us there's the company logo.

The wall is grey. The carpeting is grey. The furniture is grey. One of the suspended ceiling panels has water damage. My colleague helps herself to a Coke Light. The manager takes notes. A mobile phone vibrates on the U-shaped table.

I draw a sixth cube. I'm asked what I think. I don't know what I'm being asked to think about. I really would like to take a piss. I'm hungry. I note: September 19 and 20, 10:30 am. I blacken the two zeros in 10:30 am. I have to buy soap, orange juice, and coffee on my way home this evening. Are we the 26th or the 27th?

"Thanks, everyone, you've done good work. Let's meet again next Tuesday, same time, and we'll see how far along we are."

28

OUR SAVIOUR

In 1927, the Olympic hero becomes a national hero. As he's training in Lake Michigan with his brother, who trails him in a rowboat, a boatload of tourists capsizes a few hundred meters from the two men. With Johnny swimming, Peter rowing, they arrive at the sinking vessel in minutes, and Johnny dives down and comes back up as often as he can. That day, he saves four women, three men, and two children from certain drowning.

100% FOR WHAT'S IN YOUR MOUTH

Between 1892 and 1954, more than twelve million immigrants stopped off there. In the shadow of the Statue of Liberty sits Ellis Island.

First- and second-class passengers didn't need to stop at Ellis Island. A simple verification of passports onboard sufficed. Those who could pay for first and second class were also rich enough to pay for their own needs. America accepted them with open arms; they weren't going to become a burden for the State.

For remaining passengers, on the other hand, it was a different story. Once the ship had docked in New York's port, and after the firsts and seconds had disembarked, barges arrived to take the poor and derelict to pass medical exams.

Under military order, Europe's poor were subjected to sanitary inspections and had to bend their bodies to the logic of the Administration. On average, the proportion of people refused hovered around 2%. But when those odds fall on you, it's 100% for what's in your mouth.

WITHOUT LAKE MICHIGAN

Without Lake Michigan, Johnny Weissmuller would've never won three gold medals at the Paris Olympics in 1924. If a Métis and an Amerindian hadn't set up a trading post at the lip of a fabulous lake in the middle of nowhere, Johnny Weissmuller wouldn't have brought home two gold medals from Amsterdam in 1928. If the first American settlers hadn't built Chicago on the shores of Lake Michigan, Johnny Weissmuller, born János, would've never become Tarzan. He would have never found himself at the bottom of a swimming pool with a nude Maureen O'Sullivan, before W.S. Van Dyke's camera. He would have never been riddled with guilt about the death of Lupe Vélez. He would've never drunk whisky with Humphrey Bogart and John Wayne on Sunday afternoon at the Yacht Club in Beverly Hills. If Louis Jolliet hadn't taken part in the discovery of the Mississippi, Peter Weissmuller, Johnny's father, would've never left home to discover the New World. Without Lake Michigan and the white man, Peter wouldn't have quit the mine to go open a bar in Chicago. He would've never become an alcoholic, never beaten his wife in front of his son, who ran away to sleep under the 17th Avenue train bridge.

They never spoke again. When Johnny was twelve years old, his mother told him that his father was dead. That day, while playing knights and imitating Douglas Fairbanks leaping from a lookout tower onto a draw-bridge, Johnny fell on a fencepost that pierced into him just under his throat and broke his arm. After six months of not being able to speak, Johnny found himself with a really high-pitched voice. His vocal chords had been damaged. But, thanks to this handicap, he landed his first job on the streets of Chicago. This kid who was only twelve was able to make his own money for the first time by working at the corner vegetable trolley. Standing in front of the cart, Johnny trumpeted with all his might the prices and bargains to be had that day. His piercing squeal could unfortunately be heard across the entire neighborhood. The shop-keep saw his sales rise day by day. Above all, some customers bought vegetables simply so the boy would shut up and take his squeals elsewhere. It was unbearable, that voice; in the end, he even woke up my youngest who was barely three months old. He who already sleeps so little. His father works all night, during the day he needs his rest.

Some years later, he can be found at a hotel in Down-town Chicago, where he's the bellboy. But when he was not shouting at the top of his lungs in front of the vege-table cart or pressing an elevator button, Johnny was swimming with his little brother, Junior. From June to September, they lived in the icy waters of Lake Michigan.

Their members, aching from the frigid waters, preferred this caress to the rigors of the outside world. Floating, diving, turning onto their backs, rolling, letting themselves sink, lurching for-ward first with one arm then with both. Challenges set up between friends were a joy, even if it was a bygone conclusion that Johnny would win yet again. One day someone suggested he come train at the YMCA pool. He spent two hours in the water every day. He swam fast, really fast. He ended up being introduced to Big Bill Bachrach, star coach of the Chicago swim team. Bachrach trained the best, the heroes of a young America in search of new gods capable of incarnating the nation beyond its frontiers. Ed Bachrach wanted to go to the Olympic Games. It was his life's ultimate goal, the Olympic Games. To be the best in the world, an enviable vantage point. He would've never made it without Lake Michigan.

31

LA VIDA NO VALE NADA

Today we went to see the circus. A circus without animals. There was a clown, acrobats, and a trapeze artist. There was also a ballerina, a prehistoric man, and a ringmaster. The people there laughed and applauded. For the final act, they all held their breaths when an acrobat, tethered only at the ankles, dove toward the ground.

When we got out, my son had earned himself a Coke. The artists were selling posters and they looked worn out. We went home and prepared a meal. We ate it while watching episodes of Bugs Bunny on YouTube. The circus and Bugs Bunny have a lot in common. I wonder if we could train a rabbit for the circus? I try to imagine a training session with a rabbit. The rabbit turns in a circle, eats a carrot, while the trainer and his whip get nowhere. He runs after the rabbit and that makes the children laugh. Then he pulls out a stuffed toy, a female rabbit, to catch its attention. But this circus rabbit is well trained, it feigns disinterest. So then the trainer pulls out a stuffed fox to scare this rabbit that won't flinch. He pretends the fox is devouring the female rabbit. At this point, the rabbit can't take it anymore; he attacks the trainer. The crowd goes delirious.

32

VILLAJOYOSA

Toward the end of the nineties, I lived in a neighborhood of gypsies. Out the kitchen window we saw women sunning themselves. Bohemian grannies and teens in deep discussion. A cocky young man occasionally stopping by on a scooter or motorcycle. The heat was humid along the coast of the Mediterranean in July, in the southeast of Spain.

I can no longer keep quiet / I can no longer live like this / because I can't / because, even if God wants it, I don't / because I can no longer, ah, because I can no longer, ah / because I can no longer live without her // I'm a gypsy and I'm coming to your weddings / to tear off my shirt / I'm a gypsy and I'm coming to your weddings / to tear off this shirt that they've stained.

–Camarón de la Isla, *Soy Gitano*

33

TEN THOUSAND DOLLARS

After his Olympic career, Johnny starts working profes-
sionally for BVD swimwear. He performs at aquatic
trade-shows, at that time the equivalent of being on the
big-screen with a Dolby Surround Stereo System. People
come to see swimming events that feature dozens of performances. There's diving, synchronized swimming, speed
races, mermaids who jump into the water while wearing
white ostrich feathers in dazzling arrays on their heads.
America in the thirties, the extravagances of a nation rich
and sure of itself. Already powerful but not yet arrogant.
Already too pleased with its beliefs to continue living in
its illusion of a New World. The America of AquaCad,
the nation that developed it. America, an event. Beyond
the West, in need of a new conquest. That's where
Hollywood comes in.

On February 28, 1931, Johnny briefly marries a woman named Bobbe. Unfortunately for her, shortly after,
Hollywood digs its hook into her man. And one of the
conditions that MGM imposes on the contract is that
Johnny be single. The young girls who see him on the big

screen must believe that they can one day find themselves in his arms, become the woman in his life, his better half. But here, our good-natured Big John slams the door. Turns out it was the first time in the history of the majors that someone refused a contract for five hundred dollars per week to make movies. But the studios hadn't had their final word. The handlers went and found Bobbe, Weissmuller's young wife, and let it be known that if she played along, Hollywood would put its weight behind her budding career as a singer. And they would also pay her a ten thousand dollar advance once the divorce was final. It was the type of proposition that couldn't be refused, unless you didn't know what was good for you.

When Weissmuller appeared for the first time on the screens along Hollywood Boulevard, surrounded by jungle and embracing Maureen O'Sullivan, Bobbe was sipping her first whiskys in Las Vegas with businessmen who were really very very nice.

34

SYMBOLS

Galileo's stake, Newton's apple, Benjamin Franklin's kite, Kennedy's bullet, Armstrong's footprint, Jean Paul's pope mobile, Mao's red book, Christ's cross, Volta's frog, Che's beret, Lenin's goatee, Napoleon's hand in the vest, Mallarmé's dice, Kerouac's road, Wilde's portrait, Bogart's trench coat, James Dean's Porsche, Einstein's formula, Marilyn and her subway grate, Woody Allen and his Brooklyn bridge, Néron's lyre, the Beatles' haircuts, Tintin and Milou, Caesar's laurel wreath, Chaplin's cane.

Tarzan and Cheeta, Jane, a lion, a crocodile, vines, elephants, and a cry that was heard across the ages, from our childhood dreams.

35

LOLLIPOP

Better to be where things are really good. Like in your arms for example. Doing nothing, my love, not even feeling the urge to write. Simply nestling your breast, happy.

36

SAMUEL DE CHAMPLAIN

It's lasted for weeks. The fever isn't letting up. We continue to boil him birch bark. When he opens his eyes, everything spins. He believes all over again that he's on the Atlantic. He's crossed the oceans too many times, twenty voyages in thirty years. In his lucid moments, he obsesses over his first voyage. He says that on that day, in the year of our Lord 1603, he would've perhaps been better off staying in Brouage.

There was a storm at the mouth of the big river, whales in the hundreds, the wild coast, Indians, and his first winter in Canada. Many had followed him, many men and women to form this colony, to found this city of Quebec in 1608.

He had walked all the way to the Great Lakes, but now his legs could no longer move. Paralysis sets in. On Christmas Day, it wins out. Champlain dies. The year is 1635, Rembrandt paints *Belshazzar's Feast*. Merry Christmas. Today, because of Cartier and Champlain, millions of Quebecers curse the cold, snow, and winter.

37

BETTER OFF STAYING IN BED

We wake up with swollen eyes. We can't get ourselves to admit that we have to get out of bed. We don't know why. If it's raining outside, all the better. If it's sunny, we'd feel even worse. We look around, wondering to ourselves what we can do here, without leaving. It's our bedroom, but it could just as well be that of someone else's, it doesn't matter. The day will be long. How can we get by without coffee? So arrives the moment when we get dressed, and it's here we crack, because we're com-pelled to look at ourselves in the mirror, because our eyes fill with disgust at the sight of these hideous faces, whose paths we would never care to cross.

38

VISITATION RIGHTS

In 1948, his accountant delivers some bad news: "Johnny, you don't have a penny left! You're ruined!" The best-paid actor in the world had run out of money. It was all gone. After the champagne, the parties, the girls, the yachts, the house on Sunset Boulevard, the three pools, the first-class flights on Pan Am, it was over. Beryl, his third wife, had closed her eyes to his Hollywood debaucheries. But bankruptcy is the drop of water that overflows the vase. She asks for a divorce. Given her husband's affairs and alcoholism, her request is easily granted, along with custody of their three children: Johnny Junior, Wendy, and Heidi. Their father has no right to see them without the authorization of his ex-wife, that is to say if she telephones the court to say that he can come claim them. If he shows up unauthorized, he could end up in jail. Beryl would very much like to see him behind bars for a while, just for fun, just to get back at him a little.

So, every Sunday, she dresses up her three children and tells them that, today, their father is coming to see them. She instructs them to go sit quietly in the living room after breakfast, because he should be arriving soon.

During this time, every Sunday, Johnny goes to the court to find out if his ex has sent along the proper authorization. Every Sunday, one court clerk or another tells him no. They could've gone to amusement parks, to the beach, the movies...

When Weissmuller shared these truths with his son, who was by then in his forties, the latter fell into the most overwhelming sadness he'd ever experienced. All his life, he'd resented his father. His stomach had rattled with the hope that his father would be there on those innumerable missed Sundays, a hope that Tarzan would finally come for him, him and his sisters, for an unforgettable day. That day never arrived. His mother had simply used them. They were her bait. She wanted Tarzan to show up unauthorized to further ensnare him. When Junior saw Johnny Sheffield on the screen, between Tarzan and Jane, he bawled. Why could Tarzan have a son, but not Weissmuller?

39

JFK

John Fitzgerald Kennedy had said of Ellis Island, "There were probably as many reasons for coming to America as there were people who came."

Religious persecution, the hazards of life, unemployment, family, a desire for adventure, those were the reasons for the largest migration in the history of humanity. From 1892, the majority of immigrants, twelve million, gained entry to American life through this island. Today, Ellis Island is a museum in the memories of all those who made this nation their adopted home.

New York's JFK airport receives on average fifty million travellers per year. The last time I passed through JFK, it was to attend a convention in New Jersey. We landed, I waited my turn to pass through customs, show my passport, answer questions. My phone rang, I answered, and I saw a gorilla in uniform throw himself on me while shouting, "Turn off that phone immediately! Turn it off right now!" In that moment of surprise, I hesitated. He got me in a stranglehold, I found myself being knocked to the ground. When I recounted the story to my American colleagues, it seemed normal to them.

After customs at JFK, these words from the Declaration of Independence are engraved in gold letters on a faux-marble plaque bolted to the wall: "All men are created equal; they are endowed by their Creator with certain unalienable Rights; among these are Life, Liberty, and the pursuit of Happiness." Welcome to America.

40

JUNGLE HUT, INC.

At the beginning of 1969, an idea that had been kicking around for a while in Johnny's head takes shape. He gives it a name: Jungle Hut, Inc. He hopes to branch it out into four ventures: Jungle Hut restaurants, Johnny Weissmuller fruits and vegetable markets, Johnny Weissmuller's Safari Hut gift shops, and the Johnny Weissmuller Ungawa Club Lounges. But apart from a few health-product shops in Los Angeles, St. Louis and Chicago, the multinational effort crashes before taking off.

In 1973, Johnny Weissmuller hits rock bottom. He's on his fifth marriage, and his accountant has long ago run off with his savings. He's aged, he's put on weight, he has white hairs, a double chin, and only faded glory. He has a few galas left to host. He participates in a special day in San Antonio reuniting all the actors who ever played Tarzan on the screen. For the official photo, they're all dressed up in animal skins and made to smile. It's pathetic. They're old and tired but the reflex is still there, and that's what makes the photo so pitiful, this gathering of men who are now too old: they'd tasted the pleasures of adulation, they were sex symbols. Thirty years later, in their smiles and poses they express always and again the regret of no longer being, or having been and being no longer. It's really quite repulsive to become a celebrity. It's like the photos of old movie actresses who've had hundreds of facelifts and still believe that they can stand before the camera, without eliciting a profound sense of repulsion from those who watch them.

After the galas and official openings of municipal pools, Johnny takes a job as a host at Caesars Palace. At the time, it's the biggest hotel in Las Vegas, but he's only there to do minor walk-on appearances. He's there to get people chattering: "Did you see that? That was Tarzan who said hello and gave us our menus. Imagine that, at Caesars Palace they can afford to pay the one, the true, the only Tarzan!"

People don't know that Weissmuller is ruined. They don't know that he played Jungle Jim all those years just to pay rent. He has nothing to look forward to ahead of him. He's at Caesars not to amuse himself, but to survive.

One crowd-filled evening, his foot gets caught in the carpet. He falls and fractures a hip. It's the beginning of a long series of health problems.

We've recounted a book's worth of stories about the life of this long-gone Olympic champion and star of cinematic history. Some among them are as they actually hap-pened, while others have been shaped. The one that happened in Cuba is somewhere in between.

A golf tournament for old movie stars is organized in Havana. We're in 1959. Castro has been in power for four months, and the American embargo is not yet part of the forecast. Weissmuller and his teammates are on route to the golf course but Cuban rebels, machine-guns in hand, stop their car. Weissmuller has but the one reflex, he unleashes his famous Tarzan cry, which is as much a part of his legend as his muscles and his ability to part waters. The rebels, after several seconds of surprise and hesitation, recognize this hero of the big screen. So, as proud as peacocks, they escort Weissmuller and his pals to the golf course. We'll ignore that, at this very moment, Castro is meeting with Vice President Richard Nixon at the White House, as opposed to Eisenhower, who can't be there on the pretext of an important golf game. He leaves it to Nixon to find out if the Líder Máximo is a communist.

Johnny also has another business idea in mind: a tropical Wonderland in Titusville, Florida, that would house a snake farm, a petting zoo, and a clothing store. But this project doesn't get off the ground any more successfully than the others.

41

CARNAGE

I was twelve years old, I had a bow and arrows. With my mother and grandmother, my aunt and uncle, we went for a walk in a forest near my grandfather's sugar shack. It was summer, a beautiful day, and I was a hunter in search of prey.

Around a large cord of wood, a throng of squirrels dispersed in all directions, running here, climbing there, burrowing in hollows, scurrying along trunks and fluttering through the leaves. They were a marvel to watch, but I had a bow and arrows. The first one got lost as I overshot it into the distance. The second pegged a squirrel to a tree trunk not five meters from where I stood. I screamed. The squirrel struggled, scratched at the maple's trunk with my arrow in its back.

My uncle crushed the animal with his boot to put it out of its misery.

These days, I'm a waiter at a hip restaurant in Montreal.

42

HIROSHIMA

When Louis Réard wants to launch his brand-new bathing suit, the bikini, none of the top Parisian models of the era want to jeopardize their careers by wearing a slip of fabric that barely covers anything at all. So, the job goes to a stripper from the Paris Casino. She's in the habit of having her skin seen, with or without bikini, the thought of it makes her neither hot nor cold. Her name is Michèle Bernardini, she came to Paris at the age of eighteen, etc.

That July 18th, 1946, at the Molitor pool, she's going to have her fifteen minutes of fame before Warhol even invents the concept. The place is packed. She poses before journalists. The strips of fabrics that cover Michèle Bernardini's breasts, pelvis, and behind can fit inside a single matchbox. The press goes crazy. "The first anatomic bomb," as it later says in the advertising. The next day's news-papers disparage the obscenity of this new clothing that lets you see, in the grimness of the post-war period, new territory to be conquered. They can't foresee a day when all women taking to the beaches in summer would go about wearing so little. By baptizing his creation with the name of the atoll where humanity's most destructive weaponry was detonated, he creates a massive weapon for peace. The day they can watch women walking around in bikinis, men will forget about making war. It doesn't last for long. The bikini is banned from all beaches in France, Spain, and Italy. The world has to wait for Brigitte Bardot in a gingham bikini for the ban to finally crumble.

The day after the bikini exhibit at the Molitor, certain acerbic Parisian critics write that this thing is called a bikini because that's all that was left on the bodies of survivors after the detonation of the famous bomb tested in the Marshall archipelago.

Faced with such contempt, Réard has but one response. "The bikini – smaller than the smallest bathing suits in the world."

Réard's boutique, on Avenue de l'Opéra, closed its doors the year of Weissmuller's death, in 1984.

43

WHY DO RE MI FA SOL LA SI DO?

We owe this designation of musical notation to the Tuscan monk Guido of Arezzo, who fixed the exact pitch of each sound and gave them their names, by taking the first syllable from the first seven verses of the following hymn to Saint John the Baptist.

Ut queant laxis
Resonare fibris
Mira gestorum
Famuli tuorum
Solve polluti
Labii reatum
Sancte **I**ohannes

(Do let our voices
resonate most purely,
miracles telling,
far greater than many;
so let our tongues be

lavish in your praises
Saint John the Baptist)

In 1673, the Italian Bononcini replaced "ut" with "do",
which had a more accurate tone.

44

THE MAN WHO NEVER LOST A RACE

I've wrestled crocodiles in the heart of Africa. I've eaten roots and danced with lions. I was born in the deep jungle, in a den of reptiles. I've eaten insects. Millions of women fall asleep at night, their imaginations overflowing with fantasies in which I swim forcefully, knife in my teeth, skin branded by the sun, braving piranhas, toward the woman of my life. A boa constrictor has coiled around her fragile body and wants only to drag her down to the bottom of the river. I cut off the head of the serpent, and we make love all night.

My name is Johnny, and I'm Tarzan the Apeman.

He was the first to swim a 100-meter freestyle in under a minute. That was on July 9, 1922. He won fifty-two US championships, and set twenty-eight world records. Johnny Weissmuller never lost a single race before he retired from the sport.

One of Johnny Weissmuller's particularities is his method of swimming the crawl with his head out of the water, a method that's since been abandoned.

45

LANGUAGE

The human condition's greatest conquest is language.
Language's greatest conquest is the human condition.

46

LUPE (OUT OF THE LOOP)

Lupe Vélez, real name María Guadalupe Vélez de Villa-lobos, was a Mexican actress better known for her tum-ultuous love life than for her acting talents. After a romance with Gary Cooper, she married Johnny Weissmuller in 1933. But Lupe drank too much, she was too sensitive, and eventually this untamable Jane turned poor Tarzan's life into a living hell. They divorced in 1939.

Lupe drinks more and more, dabbles in psycho-tropics, has panic attacks at world-class social functions in the presence of Chaplin or Fairbanks. At thirty-six years old, she finds herself pregnant by a young actor, Harald Maresch, who refuses to acknowledge the child is his. This is too much; she'd messed up her life with Gary, she'd messed up her life with Johnny, she'd messed up her life in film. Nobody appreciates her true and inestimable value. So the long-forgotten icon of darkened movie-houses, so often filmed in close-up, under a white light that formed an angelic halo around her head, decides to end it all. It would be her revenge.

One December evening, the child in her womb, she planned the whole thing. Her final role would be perfect.

Hundreds of rose bouquets perfumed her villa. She brought in her make-up artist, her hairdresser, her stylist. She prepared her last scene.

Immaculate bed linens spread just so, she could already see herself as a felled Cinderella, her arms slung low and letting fall her life's last flute of champagne.

At the beginning of the evening, she shoos away the entourage. She wants to be alone. She pours champagne and swallows pills. She would love to cry but she doesn't dare, for fear that her Rimmel will run. And she stretches out, her head rested high atop a mountain of pillows. And she holds back more tears. And she drinks. And she takes more pills. Her head spins. She didn't think the end would be so easy. The child in her womb has practically gone numb. She can't feel it anymore. She only feels her stomach tighten. Her heartbeat quickens. All at once, panic overwhelms her when she realizes that she's going to vomit. No, it can't be, not now, not in this white dress, not with this fine powder on her cheeks. And this lipstick on her lips, and the roses, the scent of roses in her home? No, she didn't arrange all that for nothing, she has to quickly go to the bathroom. It'll pass. It's not serious.

Lupe Vélez commits suicide on December 13, 1944, at the age of thirty-six. We find her, head in a toilet bowl filled with vomit, her eyes blackened, her mouth contorted, a sneer of disgust on her face. She'd messed up her exit. The Mexican Spitfire is no more.

This Hispanic panther's suicide also marked the end of the young actor Harald Maresch's career. The American public couldn't forgive him for the suicide of a pregnant actress. How could he have refused to marry such an angelic creature?

WEISSMULLER MARRIES A GOLFER

Reno, Nevada – February 7, 1948

Five hours after divorcing Beryl Scott, his third wife, forty-three year-old Johnny (Tarzan) Weissmuller exchanges marriage vows with twenty-two year-old Allene Gates, a golf champion from Los Angeles. Earlier that afternoon, Big John was seen signing off on his divorce with the mother of his three children, after nine years of marriage.

All in all, it's Johnny's fourth marriage. His previous wives are, in order, the singer Bobbe Arnst, the sorely missed Lupe Vélez, and the socialite Beryl Scott. There were rumors of another marriage, before Bobbe Arnst, with a certain Camilla Louie, but of that there is no official record.

In any case, we can't say that all actors are superstitious. Weissmuller and his new wife flew that Friday, February 13, to London, where the swimmer took part in an aquatic gala.

48

BLACK PANTHER

Betty Leabo, better known by the name Brenda Joyce, took over from Maureen O'Sullivan at Johnny Weissmuller's side for five films in the *Tarzan* series.

Brenda is the mother of charming little Pamela. As it happens, she organized a magnificent party for her little darling's fifth birthday at her Beverly Hills home last week. The party was unfortunately cut short. Just before the cutting of the cake, Brenda showed off several photos of her last shoot with Tarzan. Upon seeing the images, her daughter Pamela went hysterical at seeing her mother chased through the jungle by an angry black panther.

Tarzan and the Huntress, produced by RKO, remained imprinted in Pamela's memories on account of that damned black panther.

49

BRAUTIGAN

The morning of October 4, 1984, Richard Brautigan woke up thinking, "Now, today feels like the kind of day that would put a bullet in someone's head." And you know what he did? He put a bullet in his head.

GENTLEMEN ONLY, LADIES FORBIDDEN

A famous photo of Weissmuller, taken just before the beginning of his downfall, shows him at forty-three years old with his young and delicious wife, the golfer Allene Gates. She's twenty-two, they're in Rome. These are among the most iridescent days of their life together. In the afternoon, Johnny swims in pools surrounded by hundreds of spectators, it's not the heights of his Olympic glory days, but it's his bread and butter. And in the evening, it's dining at sumptuous Italian restaurants. Allene wears an exorbitantly priced ermine scarf. She has hair that falls in golden waves along her fragile shoulders. Johnny has a tie on and his smile stretches from ear to ear. They're happy.

She's tomboyish. He met her on the golf course. She's the daughter of one of his partners. As a result of playing the course together, they became friendly. She was barely twenty years old, he forty, but take into account that he's the human hydroplane, an Olympic champion and, above all, an Apollo of the movie house, an Adonis with a glistening torso that millions of women around the world have dreamed of holding in their arms. How could Allene, a young Californian girl from a good family, resist? He could have been her father, but how could the champion of the California greens escape the ape man?

One Saturday afternoon at the golf club, after the eighteenth hole, before a scotch, Big John asks his partner, a respectable fifty-year-old family patriarch, for the hand of his daughter. It was their last round of golf together.

51

SHEEP

A sheep
stranded
in September

spins strangled
suits
in spring

A stranded
sheep
in spring

is strangled
into suits
come September

52

I REMEMBER

How can I say this? I've had enough of this shit. All this shit from all this information. I no longer know what direction to take with my life. My life sucks. I'm fed up. Where to start? Is it because I'm about to turn forty? Maybe it's because I've never taken enough risks. But risk what? Because I've wanted to be perfect and do as I should, I've never done anything. I've let myself be pulled into every single trick thrown at me, and now I'm full of shit. And now I'm retching. Now I'm vomiting. Now my throat's tightening. It's tying me up in knots. It's pulling my insides out. I no longer know how to go about my daily business. I no longer know anything. There's an evil swelling up inside me. It's been swelling since I was thirty, since I was twenty, for a very long time, too long. Only water and swimming lets me forget. They're the only things that help. It was along these lines of thinking that I discovered the wonders of alcohol. A raised glass to the love of forgetting. A raised glass to the art of remembering. I remember.

53

ON THE ROAD

If Kerouac managed to write *On the Road* in three weeks, after seven years of bohemian journeys, then I should be able to write *On the Highway* in one week, after nine years of traffic jams. I just have to let it come, to let the yarn unspool.

Take a breath, and bang!

54

IRIS RISK

Lisa lingered over
Lilies on the Azure
Eyes glazing.

55

1914 – 1981

I vividly remember the only time my father ever slapped me. I remember the truncated, dry sound it made. I had a numb cheek. I was twelve years old. It was summer. My buddy Donald and I were building cabins in the woods. The slap, I no longer know why, struck me like an insult. I've never come to terms with it, which is why I still remember it. In the days that followed, I had but one idea in my head: run away. Take my tent and my sleeping bag and go camp in the woods for a few days. I was obsessed with the idea. Donald wanted to come with me. We built it up in our heads. We had to do it if we were men. We didn't do it.

In Chicago on Cleveland Avenue, Johnny took his lumps weekly. His mother also took her share of punches. Johnny clenched his teeth. One day, he would kill his monster of a father. But on Chicago's Cleveland Avenue in 1914, a beat-up kid was nothing new. For me, all I got was a harmless little smack, an uncharacteristic outburst that my father regretted, and I transformed it into a big deal. That was in 1981.

56

A LONE DEFEAT

There was once a young boy named Johnny. In Chicago, in 1914, he was ten years old. His father and his mother were Hungarian immigrants. They'd passed through Ellis Island before joining family in Windber, Pennsylvania.

In God We Trust.

At ten years old, Johnny is diagnosed with poliomyelitis. At the beginning of the nineteenth century, poliomyelitis's symptoms was described successively as Dental Paralysis, Infantile Spinal Paralysis, Essential Paralysis of Children, Regressive Paralysis, Myelitis of the Anterior Horns, and Morning Paralysis. So the doctor advised his mother to get him swimming. This was how Johnny found himself at the neighborhood pool, Chicago's Stanton Park pool, every day of the week. By the time he was twelve, he swam so well that he joined the YMCA team.

On June 2, 1920, blowing out the sixteen candles on his birthday cake, Johnny wished in secret that this year would be the one he'd be able to swim for the most coveted club in the city: the Illinois Athletics Club. His wish came true a few months later when he was introduced to star trainer Ed Bachrach. The latter couldn't believe his eyes: "A stopwatch never lies!" He added: "What's more, this little guy's not even giving it all he's got!"

Johnny Weissmuller, Coach Bachrach's young prodigy, made his amateur debut on August 6, 1921, in a fifty-yard freestyle that he lost. It would be his only loss. His bathing cap had fallen into his eyes. For the next race he had the right fit, and he never lost another one. That one-hundred yard was his first competition in an Amateur Athletic Union event, the organizing body that has regulated the sport for the majority of the twentieth century.

In 1921, he was seventeen years old when he broke the world record for the hundred yard at Brighton Beach, New York. He becomes, for the era's newspapers, the dolphin man, the prince of waves, the human hydroplane, the aquatic pearl. In the Chicago of the 1920s, dominated by Al Capone, the mob, and the Black Sox scandal, Weissmuller strikes the figure of a white angel. He redeems the sins of the city in the eyes of the world.

From 1921 to 1928, Johnny won five Olympic gold medals, fifty-two national championships, sixty-seven world championships. He's also a member of the water-polo team until 1927.

Already in Weissmuller's time, science was at the service of sport. Special bicarbonate mixtures, after intensive research, neutralize acidity in the muscles, reducing fatigue, aches, and blood acidosis. Performance evaluations conducted by laboratory scientists show an improvement between 30% and 90%. This information was in *Swimming the American Crawl*, first published in 1931 but now out of print and unavailable, even on Amazon.

By the end of his Olympic glory, Johnny drops amateur swimming for a promotional contract with BVD swimwear valued at $300 per week. He's rich! He's asked to stay at five-star hotels, to swim, to have drinks with the most beautiful girls in the country, to pose practically nude in BVD bathing suits, to party, to appear perfectly content; all this for an exorbitant salary. Johnny executes, and they are the best years of his life.

Then one day he visits MGM Studios. They want him to star as a leading man opposite Maureen O'Sullivan, Mia Farrow's future mother. He's not at all an actor, his voice is too shrill and insufferable, but in this case he only has two words to say: Tarzan, Jane.

Box-office success is immediate. After the great depression, the miserable masses are transported by the story of this hero and his ability to thrive in such a natural state. Tarzan has no clothes, no weapons, no books, no work, and he's happy. He's found a lost paradise. He's pure and good. He's the supreme hero. He carries with him only the forces of life, and they sustain him.

Between 1932 and 1948, Weissmuller films ten full-length instalments of Tarzan. From *Tarzan, the Ape Man* to *Tarzan and the Mermaids*, he's the best-paid actor in Hollywood.

57

PHELPS MINUS 100

In Baltimore, Michael Phelps is born in 1985. He begins swimming at the age of seven to treat a troublesome attention deficit disorder (hyperactivity). Today, he's been entered into legend for bringing home eight gold medals at the 2008 Olympics in Beijing. Since the beginning of his career, he's won fourteen Olympic gold medals. We might say he's the top swimmer of all time, one of the top Olympic athletes. He was never able to bring home the gold in the 100-meter freestyle. It's worth noting that he didn't even try.

Here's the list of those who have done it:

Athens 1896	Alfréd Hajós
London 1908	Charles Daniels
Stockholm 1912	Duke Kahanamoku
Antwerp 1920	Duke Kahanamoku
Paris 1924	Johnny Weissmuller
Amsterdam 1928	Johnny Weissmuller
Los Angeles 1932	Yasuji Miyazaki
Berlin 1936	Ferenc Csík

London 1948	Walter Ris
Helsinki 1952	Clarke Scholes
Melbourne 1956	Jon Henricks
Rome 1960	John Devitt
Tokyo 1964	Don Schollander
Mexico 1968	Michael Wenden
Munich 1972	Mark Spitz
Montreal 1976	Jim Montgomery
Moscow 1980	Jörg Woithe
Los Angeles 1984	Rowdy Gaines
Seoul 1988	Matt Biondi
Barcelona 1992	Alexander Popov
Atlanta 1996	Alexander Popov
Sydney 2000	Pieter van den Hoogenband
Athens 2004	Pieter van den Hoogenband
Beijing 2008	Alain Bernard

The attentive reader will have remarked by now that the first swimmer in history to win gold in the 100-meter freestyle is Hungarian: Alfred Hajós. And there was Weissmuller. And finally, in 1936: Ferenc Csík, another Hungarian. I wonder, what pushed all these Hungarians to swim so fast?

58

MAPLE SYRUP

It was necessary that she make a living. It was habit that
saved her. Her body was used to breathing, her feet to
advancing one after the next, her mouth to making
sounds. Little by little, all this became second nature, even
natural. At the end of 1969 she celebrated her twenty-
fourth birthday, her first wedding anniversary, and the
first ten months of her newborn's life.

She owned a beauty salon. She taught hotel courses.
She became a restaurant manager. During this period
they were separated. I was seven years old. She went to
live with a friend in Quebec City. I stayed with my father
in the country. She found a waitressing gig in the city.

I spent all my weekends with her, in her little apartment. She came to get me Friday after school, in her blue
Renault 5. We drove the half-hour back to her one-
bedroom apartment in Sainte-Foy. We ate together or she
prepared something for me. Her shift began at 6 pm. She
tried to be back early, before midnight. I was eight years
old. I watched TV. My mom had a cable package with
eighteen American channels and I could watch *Hulk* on

WCAX Burlington. It was a black-and-white TV, without a remote control. Remote controls didn't exist back then. To change the channel, we had to get up and turn a big plastic knob with the numbers 1 through 13 and the UHF signal marked above it. When we turned that knob, it fired off as much brute noise as a Kalashnikov.

Alone in this little apartment, surrounded by the city, I was often afraid at eight years old. I was surrounded by thousands of people, me who spent the rest of the week living in the middle of the woods with my dogs, my cats, my snowshoes and my air rifle. Protected like that, I could take on the world fearlessly. But on Friday nights, at quarter-past-eleven watching *The Island of Thirty Coffins* in my mom's one-bedroom, I was scared. At the slightest noise behind the door, my heart would jump. I slept on the couch. By morning, my mom would be in her room. I could hear her get up to make my breakfast. I'd forgive her everything. Because Saturday mornings, she made me pancakes with maple syrup.

59

OLYMPIC SWIMMING CATEGORIES

The Olympic swimming categories are as follows:

Breaststroke: 100 and 200 meters
Backstroke: 100 and 200 meters
Freestyle: 50, 100, 200, 400, and 1500 meters
Butterfly: 100 and 200 meters
Medley: 200 and 400 meters
Medley Freestyle: 4 x 100 and 4 x 200 meters
Medley Relay: 4 x 100 meters

On August 21, 1972, the hundredth of a second was added to swimming's time-keeping.

60

DONE FOR TONIGHT

I'm at Pad Thai Noodle Restaurant, at the corner of 8th Avenue and 18th Street. I'm on my way back from Ground Zero. It's September 11, 2007.

I saw Trinity Church. I saw the Woolworth Building. I saw St. Paul's Chapel. I walked along Broadway. I saw the Stock Exchange. I saw City Hall. I saw thousands of stores open all night. I crossed twenty red lights and fourteen green lights. I saw three hundred twenty-four yellow cabs. I saw ATM machines on the sidewalk. I saw the scaffolding in front of stores being renovated. Through the clouds I saw the 9/11 memorial, *Tribute in Light*. I saw women and men. They walked with backpacks and handbags. I saw the dampness of the day after a rain. I saw subway grills steam up from the sidewalks. I saw several fire hydrants. I saw sidewalk newspaper boxes disemboweled, doors open. I saw the clientele of a bar leaving with their take-out in tow. I saw a bouncer built like a tank, chatting with a waiter. I saw two pretty girls in black and white dresses, looking English but they were really American. I saw their bracelets. I saw her pearl necklaces. I saw straight couples. I saw gay couples. I saw faces from far away yet from here. I saw all the faces of the world between 18th and 20th, between 42nd and 40th, between 34th and 35th, between Bleecker and Fulton, be-tween Wall Street and Trinity.

I saw a woman in a red blouse talking to a couple, he was white, she was black. I saw her shaved armpits. I saw an Indian lady with her brother; they were having a conversation on a bench near the front window. I saw Banana Republic and Gap. I saw Equinox and the New York Sports Club. I saw Helio and Citibank. I saw the New York Sightseeing Tour bus with tourists riding on its roof. I saw a young girl with long blonde hair join the Indian lady and her brother. She wears a grey t-shirt. She smiles. They're happy to cross paths. The two girls in black and white are about to finish off their spring rolls by dipping them in a slightly reddish sauce. They drink through straws. I drink my Patrón Platinum tequila. I saw a white polo t-shirt with Adidas shorts. I saw fingernails painted red. I saw turquoise earrings. I saw a necklace of amber stones. I saw candlesticks lit on tabletops, their flames lighting up the centers of urns carved to look like the baroque façade of the Gesù Nuovo church in Naples. I saw the three friends leave under a rainbow flag of gay pride. I saw the same flag hoisted in Venice against the war: *Pace!* I saw Wild Diesel Knight 1978 on his red back. I saw her fake necklace of glass pearls. She has dirty blonde hair, she wears black-rimmed glasses and she eats with red chopsticks. Under the table, I saw her waxed right leg crossed over her left leg. I saw her curl her toe. I saw her adjust her mid-sized white belt. I saw her bring her mobile phone to her right ear. I saw her black skirt as she came back from the washroom. I saw that she looked at me. I saw that her right ear wasn't beautiful, too large. I saw my neighbor on the left get up to use the washroom. I saw the girl to my right look into her purse. I saw white dots on the blouse of the neighbor who stayed behind. I saw the washroom door open and, behind it, a mirror. I almost saw myself in it. I saw the humid watermark my tequila glass left on the oval wood table. I saw their plate of Pad Thai arrive. I saw her squeeze lime over the dish. I saw her pass her right hand along the back of her head, through her hair. I saw them talking. I saw the man facing her get up to pay. I saw the waiter forget something, leave, and then return with the bill folded into a brown faux-leather folder. I saw the MasterCard logo. I saw her sip from a straw, her eyes looking up at the ceiling as if seeking approval. I saw the waiter throw a towel in the kitchen. I saw him come back from the washroom. I saw him try to pick off a wad of paper stuck to his shoe.

I saw a No Parking 7 AM – 10 AM, MON – FRI sign tremble as a subway train rumbled below and then a truck passed by. I saw a couple, the woman with a baby in her arms. I saw that it was 10:25 pm. I saw them leave. I saw the bottom of my tequila glass. I saw the cook come back after stepping outside to have a look at the city bustle along the sidewalk. I saw a senior in a pink t-shirt using a red golf umbrella as a cane. I saw that the ice cubes in my water glass had completely melted away. I saw bubbles of condensation. I saw the number 19 emblazoned in black characters on the back of a t-shirt. I saw the boss behind the cash register. I saw the dishwasher with a Yankees cap on backwards. In the space of ten seconds, I saw nine cabs, a bus, and a Hummer pass by. I saw the lights fade. I saw another couple prepare to leave. I saw two women on the sidewalk. I saw that they had almost finished their Pad Thai. I saw the waiter removing candlesticks from the middle of the oval wooden tables. I saw the woman in a grey blouse pulling out some green bills, but those colors could have been inversed. I saw her fold her napkin after removing it from her lap, and then set it back on the table. One hand in her hair. I saw a cab stop for someone. I saw her make a phone call. I saw the waiter ask me, "The check?" I saw the lights twisting above the bar in silver pendants. I saw two immense palm leaves posed in a vase at the end of the bar. I saw the waiter leave with my AMEX. I saw a black man with iPod headphones dangling from his ears. I saw a white woman with a Duane Reade bag. I saw that I'd better go, that it was all wrapping up, that I was done for tonight.

61

PAPER JAM

The color photocopier
grays into dirty cream
flashes: paper jam.

62

PIECES

On February 14, 2009, at six in the morning, Gabriel Rivages gets into his car. He takes the on-ramp and gets on the highway. He drives faster and faster. Arriving under a bridge some 14 km from his home, he turns the steering wheel and propels the car, at a speed of 178 km/h, into the central pillar of the viaduct. The emergency crews spend hours gathering all the pieces.

63

WELCOME TO WINDOWS

Designed for Microsoft

Copyright © Microsoft Corporation

Welcome to Windows

Press Ctrl-Alt-Del to Start

Using this combination of keys at start-up permits the securitization of your computer. To obtain more information, click on Help.

User: rivages

Password: 9%tarZan!

64

WALK OF FAME

We got to Venice Beach around noon, in the rain. We dropped off our bags at the hotel and walked to the beach. We found a restaurant: The Whaler. I had a Moby Dick burger, and my two colleagues had fish 'n' chips. The rain stopped. Palm trees swayed in the wind like mohawked punks in a trance. To see trees that thin, that tall, bend like that in a storm, I figured their roots had to be dug in very deep. I would research it on Wikipedia.

That's where my journey really began: http://www. wikipedia.org.fr.request_los _angeles.htm.

Los Angeles, showbiz capital, second biggest city in the United States after New York. An agglomeration of seventeen million residents. The story of the City of Angels begins in 1850, after it was annexed to the United States following the war with Mexico. The gold rush contributed to her rise, but it was the movies that really made her what she is today: the capital of the seventh art form, the home of the film industry. Life has a way of being ubiquitously splendid, the light is ideal, and there are many shooting locations, from green meadows to glowing deserts. The aviation industry also set up their headquarters there because the exceptional weather conditions made it possible to run test flights every day of the year.

We landed at the Los Angeles airport at 2:03 pm. My first human contact with a Californian was a customs agent. I placed my left index finger on a digital print screen, I maintained the serious demeanor of someone beyond reproach as I stood before the webcam that took my photo. He asked where I was going, how long I'd be there, the reasons for my visit. What does my company make exactly? Did it have factories in China? If that was the case, he informed me that he wouldn't be able to buy our products. The Chinese know nothing about quality. Instead of goodbye, he said, "Good luck!"

My suitcase emerged quickly on the baggage claim's treadmill, as did those of my colleagues. Once we were outside, we followed the Car Rental signs to the shuttles that took us to the car-rental companies.

The bus dropped us off at the Hertz parking lot, and we found our way to the reception office. At the entrance, a young man in his twenties, a Kurt Cobain lookalike, was wearing a hat made of balloons. On his belt hung a bicycle pump and dozens of ribbed condoms. He offered balloon animals to kids. But since there weren't a lot of kids renting cars at the Los Angeles airport, he was bored. It's the kind of detail the manager of the establishment should have considered, I said to no one in particular. In the end, Kurt made a flower-shaped bracelet out of balloons for my colleague, which she admired on her wrist. Inside, my other colleague was at the counter, asking to break a twenty so that he could buy a Diet Coke from one of the innumerable vending machines in the reception area. There weren't that many people at Hertz, but there were at least a dozen vending machines where you could buy energy drinks, soft drinks, chips, chocolate, candy, chewing gum, coffee, tea, nuts, candies filled with chocolate or vitamins, dried fruit, SlimWeights, Crispies, 20% Mores, Spidermen.

Welcome

Press

Zero

Your Name

Pound Key

Five

Six

Unavailable

We did not understand your answer

You can return to the main menu at any time by pressing zero

Three

Two

Thank you

Calculating route

We were off, one eye on the road, the other on the little red GPS arrow. We sped up to 130 km/h on Interstate 10, in the direction of Country Drive Road, Palm Desert, California, USA.

The 180 kilometers that separate Los Angeles from Palm Springs are absolutely monotonous. With the exception of one or two sets left behind by westerns and the mythic wind farms immortalized in Hollywood classics, there's nothing. We saw nothing but electrical poles, highway ramps, cars, trucks, billboards ten metres tall by forty meters wide: VERIZON, BURGERS, HOME APPLIANCE, MILLER, FRIDAY 9:00PM, REAL ESTATE, CASINO...

I thought that the hotel, given how big it looked on the website, would stand out in the night. But we saw nothing at all from the main road, just a long and winding driveway lined by palm trees, just like in the American dream. Well-lit undergrowth, a majestic hall of stone and glass, valets in white, with or without caps, and Good evening, Sir, and Good evening, Ma'am, and May I take care of your suitcase?

After the conference, I treated myself to some tourism in the form of a guided bus tour. They took us to see Venice Beach, Mulholland Drive, Bob Hope's house, the Eagles' Hotel California, Beverly Hills, Rodeo Drive. At noon we drove up in front of the Kodak Theatre, where the Oscars are hosted every year. We had an hour of free time on the Walk of Fame. I walked around for a bit. When I arrived in front of 6541, I found what I was looking for. I hadn't put myself through twelve hours in planes and two days of American-style motivational meetings for nothing. I was here. I was in front of 6541 Hollywood Boulevard. Under my feet, on the Walk of Fame, there was Johnny Weissmuller's star.

65

IN PLAY

Playing
with falling
debris

I gain
the upper hand
and throw in the towel

66

ONE-WAY TICKET

We made a date for Tuesday at noon. I passed by to pick her up at her Champlain Street apartment. We went to have a drink at an outdoor patio on Cartier. It was a beautiful, sunny day at the end of August in Quebec City. I told her how I was in love, how everything else had become secondary: university, the doctorate, the career, family, friends. I was taking a plane in two days. I was going to be with her in France. I had a one-way ticket. We said goodbye without tears. We knew it was the end. We also knew it was better for everyone this way. It hurt her, but she understood. She said, "Good luck, my son."

67

GAAAAAARRRRRRYYYYYY

"Gary! Gaaaaaarrrrrryyyyyy... Gary!"

Lupe Vélez, before marrying John Weissmuller, was Gary Cooper's girlfriend. After all the crises, the fights, the clawing, and the bottles shattered against walls, Cooper had enough, and the Mexican beauty found herself in the arms of Tarzan.

Once their nuptials are consummated, the new Hollywood it-couple build a magnificent villa. When they move in, Lupe brings along nothing from her old life, with one exception: the ultimate Gary souvenir that she wanted more than anything, Jacky the parrot.

And Jacky, having spent many months amidst fights between Vélez and Cooper, has learned quite perfectly how to say, "Gary! Gaaaaaarrrrrryyyyyy... Gary!" And the bird repeats the name ad nauseam, especially when it sees a big man approach. All of which is to say that, every evening when Weissmuller returns from a shoot, comes home from a night out, steps in from a swimming gala, he's greeted by the very expensive Jacky crying, "Gary! Gaaaaaarrrrrryyyyyy... Gary!"

Little by little, Johnny begins to crack. He's been married to The Mexican Spitfire for only a year, and already the fights are inescapable. How many times has Lupe said that with Gary it wasn't like that, or Gary was like this, and at least he was a real actor, and he and he and he and he and all the while Jacky's shrieking, "Gary! Gaaaaaarrrrrryyyyyy... Gary!"

Weissmuller wouldn't have a hurt a fly. He loved animals. He spent the majority of his time with them. Between elephants, crocodiles, lions, and Cheeta, the Tarzan sets looked more like a circus tent than a film shoot. At home, Johnny had for many years owned a superb Labrador, which surely enough Lupe couldn't tolerate. One evening, upon returning home from a shoot, Samy hadn't come to rub up against his legs with its tail wagging. Johnny understood right away that Lupe had committed an irreparable offense. At that moment Jacky chose to once again project her ardent "Gary! Gaaaaaarrrrrryyyyyy... Gary!"

When Lupe returned from her dinner in the city, Jacky was no more than a bag of feathers on the living room carpet. Lupe Vélez and Johnny Weissmuller's divorce was announced on December 13, 1939.

68

ELECTRIC THEATRE

Tally's Electric Theatre is the first cinema of all time. It opened its doors in 1902 in Los Angeles. In the year that Zola died of asphyxiation from a stupid chimney fire (was it really an accident?), the world's first cinema opened its doors to its first audiences. At the time, Peter Weissmuller is a soldier in the army of Austrian emperor Franz Joseph I.

For that first screening, a seat goes for five cents. For that price, you have the right to watch life projected onto a white screen in a black room. It's like theatre, but more boring. However, if you so desire, you can pay thirty cents, and then you have access to the royal treatment. Instead of having to sit in the screening room, you can settle in behind the screen itself. There you'll have little holes through which you can watch those who are watching. These are known as "peep holes". From the very first days of cinema, voyeurism is part of the pleasure, made more profound by the technical environment of this new medium. For thirty cents instead of five, you get to watch without being seen. You can scrutinize all the faces lit up by the light's reflection on the screen, see their laughter and tears without their ever becoming aware that there are eyes behind the dream curtain, captivated by their every movement. The electric theatre was initially an inverse screening, then, like standing in between two mirrors.

69

IN BED

Rice
in milk
in bed

a little
for you
in bed

we read
we laugh
in bed

70

LAST PLUNGE

Gabriel Rivages is born the day the Québec Liberation Front sets off a bomb at the Montreal Stock Exchange. Jean-Jacques Bertrand of the Union Nationale party was Quebec's premier. Pierre Elliott Trudeau of the Liberal party was Canada's prime minister.

On that day, it wasn't only the FLQ's bombs that were exploding. Amidst the soft snowflakes of February falling over Quebec City, a woman threw herself from the fifth floor of a hospital. She'd gone there to give birth. She'd been in labor for 18 hours. She didn't want this child. It had gone much further than she'd wanted. She had the misfortune of becoming pregnant. She worked in the middle of a national park, in the only restaurant for hundreds of kilometers around. When she went back home for a few days in the summer of 1968, she was still vomiting. She didn't know what to do.

It's snowing over Quebec City. She watches the flakes disappear toward the ground. The snow falls. And because watching snow come down has a hypnotic power, she begins to feel light herself. This life that had supported two instead of one for the past nine months couldn't hold out any longer, nor did she want it to. While entranced by the snow, she began to dream of a lighter, softer existence. She imagined her childhood without her father abusing her mother, without the mocking smiles of others, without the raging outbursts followed by weeks of silence, simply to punish, to make her feel horrid, to hurt her. She forgot the stunted desires, all that envy she felt for other lives. She simply saw snow, and the pain to come. The next convulsion, the next kick. Because this child was punishing her, was making her feel worse. It was getting its revenge one last time. Here and now, it was going to make her pay for the past nine months of saying: I don't want a child.

So she got herself out of bed. She removed the identification bracelet from her wrist. She tore off her hospital gown. She backed up as far as the room would allow and then flew forward in abandon. She ran and, with a quick twist, threw herself into the glass. Her back hit the bay window, and it shattered into thousands of pieces. From that vantage point, tumbling down backward, she could watch the snow falling one last time.

71

DUMMY TEXT

Lorem ipsum dolor sit amet, consectetuer adipiscing elit. Sed non libero eu purus porttitor tincidunt. Vivamus quis ipsum. Sed nec eros a nisl feugiat vestibulum. Mauris vestibulum, velit a posuere laoreet, tortor tortor molestie mi, tempus elementum turpis quam nec metus. Aliquam metus. Fusce turpis tortor, feugiat sed, pellentesque a, rutrum id, turpis. Aenean at lacus. Morbi augue libero, volutpat aliquet, posuere nec, vulputate consequat, augue. Sed a dolor. Ut dignissim. Pellentesque sapien. Quisque ut mi sit amet libero tempor adipiscing. Curabitur bibendum. Aliquam erat volutpat. Aliquam eget mauris a diam congue venenatis. Aliquam a arcu ut quam mollis bibendum. Fusce sed tortor ornare velit sollicitudin accumsan.

"There exists no person who enjoys pain for itself, nor who seeks pain out, nor who desires pain because it is pain."

—Cicero

72

JACKPOT

Thanks to his son-in-law, when he's at his lowest in 1973, Johnny lands a job as a host at Caesars Palace in Las Vegas. He looks after rich people who want to dine at a classy restaurant while visiting the U.S. city better known as the biggest open-sky bordello in the world. The city of money, sex, excess, but Johnny is no longer capable of enjoying any of it. We know that he's fractured his hip, and that this is where the end begins. As the saying goes: "What happens in Vegas stays in Vegas."

What strikes me most when arriving by plane in Las Vegas are the slot machines. Get off the plane, and before even passing through customs, there are 150 slot machines smiling back at you. Welcome to Las Vegas, Nevada.

73

LAST BEATS FIRST

Of the three, I prefer the last:
Keats
Yeats
the Beats

74

FIRST

If you want us to remember you, then you have to be first. It's the price of entry. The best way to be first is to be first in a particular category. The best way to be first in a particular category is to invent the category. When you're first in a category, people believe in you. They say that if you're first, you must be the best. QED.

Kleenex, Frigidaire, Ski-Doo, Q-tips, andd Rolex are perfect examples of this equation. They've transformed their names into a single category, in respective order: tissue paper, refrigerators, snowmobiles, cotton swabs, and deluxe wristwatches. McDonald's became a fast-food empire by dedicating itself exclusively to hamburgers, at least initially. They created the category of "fast-food restaurant that serves only hamburgers".

The day that Johnny Weissmuller swam the 100 meter in under a minute, not only did he break a record, but he also created a new category. In the months and years that followed, the minute became the magic number to beat in his discipline. The goal of every professional swimmer became to break into the category of the 100 meter freestyle in under a minute.

When Weissmuller signed with MGM, he wasn't the first to play Burroughs's hero onscreen. Elmo Lincoln was actually the first Tarzan in 1918. But we've found another category for Weissmuller; he was the first Tarzan of the talkies. He made us hear, for the very first time, the ape man's terrible cry emanating from the depths of the jungle. Because of his cry he's become, for millions of viewers, the first Tarzan.

Lindbergh is the first man to have crossed the Atlantic by plane. In May 1927, he flew between New York and Paris in thirty-three hours aboard the *Spirit of St. Louis*. What's the name of the second man to cross the Atlantic by plane? On July 19, 1969, Neil Armstrong becomes the first man to walk on the moon. What's the name of the second?

The second athlete after Weissmuller to swim the 100 meter in under a minute has also been forgotten.

75

OLYMPUS

A shooting, cops, riot police, the military, more police, tanks, dogs, gas masks, tear gas, crowds running, crying, shots fired, people running back, beatings with sticks, jostling, tripping, cries and barked orders, fallen caps, torn jackets, a girl who grabs a leg, a punch, a camera, a street, burning cars and an ad for yogurt with honey called Sins of the Gods.

76

SAN FRANCISCO, 1931

In 1931 in San Francisco, I was at the Springsteen Hotel, Room 23. It was summer, a Saturday evening, and it was very very hot. It must've been around 11 pm. I met Jack and we had a drink together as we rolled cigarettes. He told me that his brother had lost his job at the factory; he said his wife might be cheating on him, and he told me about some work at Goldsmith & Son that he thought he could land. He was uplifting company, that Jack, and I never saw him lose his morale. His good humor and the beer, they refreshed me. I left the bar around midnight. I walked for a bit along Stockton Street before going back to my hotel room. At that moment, I heard two gunshots.

San Francisco, dark out, a Saturday night in 1931, it wasn't too shocking. But it still surprised me. I told the story to Dashiell the next day. The scene surprised me even more when I saw Bogart playing Sam Spade in *The Maltese Falcon*.

"It was impossible for me to let silence fall upon his grave without having said that."

—Aragon

77

THE INTERNATIONAL SWIMMING
HALL OF FAME

At the start of the sixties, the city of Fort Lauderdale in Florida opts to invest in an aquatic complex in order to attract tourists. Following the advice of some well-known American swimming champions, several plump bourgeois benefactors were able to extract a maximum of government funds to create the International Swimming Hall of Fame. As it happens, Americans adore sports museums.

Today, the Hall of Fame defines its mandate in the following terms:

"To promote the benefits and importance of swimming as a key to fitness, good health, quality of life, and the water safety of children."

To reach its goal, the Hall of Fame pursues the following activities:

"We will accomplish this through operation of the International Swimming Hall of Fame, a dynamic shrine dedicated to the history, memory, and recognition of the famous swimmers, divers, water polo players, synchronized swimmers, open-water swimmers, and persons involved in life-saving activities and education, throughout the world, whose lives and accomplishments will serve to inspire, educate, and be role models for all those who participate in the Hall of Fame's experience and programs."

In 1965, to inaugurate the museum, the organizers manage to convince Johnny Weissmuller to donate his most prized trophies and awards. As the highlight of the collection, Johnny bequeaths them his Olympic championship medals. Here are all the markers of his glory, brought together under one roof. For him, it doesn't matter much if his medals are in Florida or in his dining room—it's all ancient history anyhow. If he's in the Hall of Fame, all the better. He's far off from that world now.

During the Second Seminole War, between 1835 and 1840, the American army constructed a series of forts along the New River. The officer in charge of the detachment that built the first of them was named William Lauderdale. The Venice of America takes its name from him.

The years pass. And the world changes. One evening Bob puts in a phone call to Dick to say that he's dreaming of taking his son for a visit to the Swimming Hall of Fame. They have all of Johnny Weissmuller's medals there from the time he was an Olympic champion. And all those medals made of gold, they must be worth a lot. And furthermore, there aren't even guards on the premises. If you see what I'm saying? Dick replies that he sees exceptionally well what Bob means to say, that it sounds like a super plan, a golden idea.

The commandos organize. Bob and Dick visit the Hall of Fame a few times. They note the opening hours. They make sketches of the entries and exits. As for the alarm system, it's a basic model, child's play.

On a Friday at midnight, they tiptoe into the Hall of Fame as quietly as they would a church. Not a person to be seen or heard. They deactivate the alarm. They have all the time in the world, and they take it. They take all the medals and small trophies, the bigger ones won't fit through the basement window.

A few days later Bob and Dick are faced with the question of how to convert the gold into bills. It was something that they hadn't really considered before. Of course, they were elated, they had in their possession the gold medal that the French president had slipped around Weissmuller's neck in 1924, they had in their possession the gold medal that the Dutch queen had slipped around Weissmuller's neck in 1928. But that doesn't put too much butter on your bread. They can't find anyone besides one car dealer, who's willing to trade them a Ford Mustang for a gold medal from the Amsterdam Olympics. Even if it had once belonged to the great Tarzan.

Right around then Dick has a super idea: eBay! They can put the medals up for sale on eBay and see what they're really worth. And as expected, they find a collector there who takes the bait. He buys a first medal, then a second, etc. He authenticates each one and continues to buy the lot. When he receives an original trophy from the Amateur Athletic Union in the mail, he begins to think to himself that, all told, something fishy may be going on down there. Since he's a good American citizen, the collector phones the police. A few days later, this article lands in the newswire:

At the beginning of December 2004, a large portion of Johnny Weissmuller's trophies was stolen from the International Swimming Hall of Fame in Florida. The medals and trophies donated to the museum by Weissmuller when it first opened in 1965 are estimated to be worth $500,000. The thieves had attempted to sell the lot on eBay, where a collector, Mr. Erlinger, after having purchased numerous medals from a certain Logan, realized that the items must have been stolen. He contacted the museum and, today, thanks to the efforts of the police, the legacy of Johnny "Tarzan" Weissmuller has been returned to the Hall of Fame, with the exception of several silver cups.

78

CORKS

In 1924, at the Paris Olympics, swimmers' lanes are separated for the first time using cables supported with cork buoys. The 1924 games also mark the first time that the Olympic slogan "faster, higher, stronger" is used.

In front of thousands of spectators at the stadium in Colombes, Johnny Weissmuller, the American born in Hungary, wins the gold medal in the 100-meter freestyle. But that isn't all; he also wins the gold medal in the 400 meter freestyle and the 4x200 meter relay. In water polo, he settles for a bronze medal.

He becomes the first athlete to ever win so many medals at an Olympic games, 84 years before Michael Phelps's run.

79

CELLINI'S *PERSEUS*

Does Cellini's *Perseus* speak to you at all? For me, the first time I encountered it, I happened to be on a whaling ship in the middle of the Indian Ocean. It was shortly before 1850. I'd shipped out from Boston, still in the heights of its glory as the intellectual—and puritanical—capital of the United States. It's changed a lot since then, Boston. The last time I passed through, on my way to Lowell to see Kerouac's grave, on its main street (known as The Main) there remained only the brick exterior of the old Royal cinema, on whose screen the likes of Bogart and Bacall, Marilyn and Clark, Weissmuller and O'Sullivan first came to life.

All this is to say that Cellini was a great Italian sculptor in the 16th century, and that his Perseus is a major work rivaling the achievements of Donatello and Michelangelo, offering a multitude of points of view while showcasing a complex combination of strong lines.

As for Perseus himself, I suspect it had to be a young Greek in that marble, beautiful, big, and strong. But at the time I didn't know he was the son of Zeus and Danaë.

I have to admit that we were never very close, those two and me.

Just beneath the entry for "Celsius" in an old dictionary, there's a color photo of Cellini's *Perseus*. It's true that Cellini's *Perseus* is an amazing piece of art. Mattel practically copied it for their Barbie doll. But there isn't a Barbie head in Perseus's hands, no, there's Medusa's head. Okay, he was wearing a mask that renders him invisible, thanks to Hades, and also winged sandals. Still, killing Medusa was not an easy business.

If I'm speaking about Cellini's *Perseus* today, it's because I found her fifty years later, at Oscar Wilde's this afternoon. And I had the impression that I'd crossed paths with an old friend of mine.

80

JUNIOR

Johnny Weissmuller Junior, the son of the celebrity actor and Olympic champion, died yesterday at the age of sixty-five from liver cancer. No doubt better known for having been the son of Tarzan than for having been a longshoreman at the San Francisco port, Mr. Weissmuller had nevertheless led a very fulfilling life.

He was born in San Francisco in 1942, after his father moved there with his young wife Beryl Scott. The dolphin man had just signed an important contract with Billy Rose, for an aquatic show during the Golden Gate International Exposition celebrating the bridge of the same name. For many weeks, Johnny Weissmuller swam for thousands of onlookers who crowded the terrain of the artificial island built for the occasion.

Junior joined the marines after studying at the University of Southern California, where he was a member of the swim team. One can easily imagine the pressure. In the army, he became a diver-welder. His service over, he landed several supporting roles in TV series and amateur theatre. There's little doubt that during this period, faced with a career that was not taking off, he decided to stop walking in his father's shadow. No, his father's glory was not meant to continue, the grand story of the Weissmullers had peaked after one son. Now he had to try his hand elsewhere, forget, move on to other things. That's how he ended up a dockworker. The salary and benefits were good, and the docks as Marlon Brando had depicted them in *On the Waterfront* were long gone.

Johnny Weissmuller Junior spent a good portion of his final years trying to make sense of his own life. It's already not easy being named Junior, having the same name as your father, so imagine when that man is a god, a living legend. Not to mention that the legend finished off deflated. He took on a difficult task: writing his father's biography. Today, thanks to his son, we have the most authentic and complete portrait of the athlete who brought the ape man to life most sublimely. Junior's book was published in 2002 by ECW Press in Toronto under the title *Tarzan, My Father*.

81

THREE BODIES

Weissmuller was born three times. First on June 2, 1904, in Hungary. He was named János. Then on January 26, 1905, upon his arrival at Ellis Island, where he was given the name Johnny. Finally, twenty years later, he was traded into the Windber archives so that he could replace his brother in the city register. He became Peter Johnny, born in Pennsylvania.

To keep track of the Earth's trajectory around the sun, Newton has to ignore the presence of the moon. Newton's grand law doesn't function with more than two bodies: two punctual bodies of $M1$ and $M2$ mass pulling toward each other with force directly proportional to the product of their masses and inversely proportional to the square of the distance between them.

This law explains the movement of the planets in relation to the sun, but only if we consider each of them independently. However, Newton tried to find a solution that took into account the entire system, beginning with three bodies. But given the magnitude of the task, he backed off. He didn't possess the powers of calculation required to find the solution. Isaac decided to leave the problem to future generations.

Two centuries later, Henri Poincaré gave it a try and got stuck. He demonstrated that there is no solution. Trying to resolve the problem of three bodies leads him to conclude that fundamental indecisiveness guides the real world. It's impossible to calculate the positions of three bodies in $T+1$ time. So imagine the impossibility we find ourselves in when trying to predict the state of the universe in several thousand years! And that's a very good thing, since as Albert Jacquards puts it, "This freed the Future from manifestations of consequence formed in the Present."

82

BHOPAL

I dreamed that I was in church. It was during mass and my Aunt Adrienne was telling me that she'd lived in India for twenty years. She'd had a daughter, Solange, who'd died at the age of nineteen. She told me all this as if it was nothing, and asked me if I already knew.

My Aunt Adrienne lived with her parents until her marriage to my Uncle Adrien. They've lived on their farm for nearly sixty years. They raise cows and sell milk. They attend mass every Sunday, for over sixty years now. They have three boys. The youngest is a mechanic. The other two work on the family farm.

I don't recall my uncle and aunt ever going on vacation. I don't recall them ever playing with their kids. They worked, from morning to night. They woke up at five every morning, milked the cows at six. They groomed, cleaned, fed and looked after the well-being of the animals. They prepared the hay and cleaned the stable. Repaired the tractor. Prepared and sat down to their lunch at noon. Did the laundry. Had a snack. Cut wood. Went to the village. Milked the cows again at the end of the afternoon. Cleaned. Groomed. Had dinner. Returned to the stables for details, did those that were pressing but that they hadn't had time to do before because it all goes too quick, there's too much work, they should have more time, it goes too quick, it'll already be Christmas in a month, it's already the national holiday next week, the first frost will be here in a few days. As far as I could tell, they always seemed happy.

In my dream, my Aunt Adrienne dies in the Bhopal catastrophe on December 3, 1984. Like thirty-five thousand other people, she was asphyxiated to death by forty tons of methyl isocyanate that escaped into the air from a Union Carbide factory.

83

LAST MINUTE

Heidi, Johnny Weissmuller and Beryl Scott's daughter, was killed in a car accident at the age of nineteen. Years later, Johnny Junior christened his daughter Heidi in honor of his sister who'd disappeared too soon.

For Cheeta's seventy-fifth birthday, the retirement home for movie animals in Hollywood gave the chimpanzee a magnificent cake made by Design Cake on Coconut Avenue in Beverly Hills.

Tarzan's cry was filed as a trademark by the Edgar Rice Burroughs Society. According to some sources, the famous cry was the result of an audio mixing expert fusing together a dog's growl, a soprano's suspended trill, a pinched violin string, and a hyena howl played in reverse. Another source says it was more simply a yodel sped up and reversed. Weissmuller's account is also available; he says the cry was his own invention, based on a cry from his more youthful days selling vegetables. In 1970, invited on the Mike Douglas Show, Johnny explains that his famous cry was mixed together from three sound sources, a soprano, an alto, and the cry of a hog caller.

In the mythical scene from the first *Tarzan*, where the Beauty first meets the Beast, Weissmuller never said, "Me Tarzan, you Jane." He'd simply said, "Tarzan, Jane." Brave Johnny recounted his contempt on this subject to his friend Bogart, who replied, "You're driving yourself mad. What counts is that the public believes it. You know, I never said, 'Play it again, Sam.'"

Mark Goodman said Weissmuller's story should be read by every person who wanted to have a career in the movies. It's the perfect manual of everything you should avoid so that you won't be totally exploited and then discarded like an old sock. Goodman was one of MTV's first five VJs. He launched the channel on August 1, 1981, presenting "Video Killed the Radio Star" by The Buggles.

Johnny Weissmuller was born János, and if we invert the vowels, that makes Jonas. For a swimming champion to end up in the belly of a whale, I'd say that evens things out.

84

PAPER MATE 0.5 BLACK

I don't know why. I don't pay attention to where it comes from. Ever since I was a teenager, I've written. I have this cursed need to write that won't leave me. As it happens, in this very moment, I'm on the patio of a café, having a beer—and I'm writing. I could content myself with eyeing the passing girls. I could read the newspaper. I could go back to work or go home. But no, I choose to write. I want to write. I need to write. I have this need and I know, no matter what I write, no matter when I stop, I'll feel better. It's not simply a matter of putting down crap with hot ink, no: truly, physically, I feel better for doing it. It calms me. It empties me. When I have concerns, when I become obsessed, when my life turns damp and drizzly, I pick up a pen and it replaces thoughts of suicide. "This is my substitute for pistol and ball." Caton throws himself on his sword; I write.

I write also in happiness. It happens. If I could, I would write all the time. I exaggerate. I tell myself often that it will all be for nothing. That it's garbage. And I stop writing, I toss out my notebooks, I erase my documents.

Until the next crisis. Until that instant when it takes hold of my solar plexus, when I begin to experience migraines ad nauseam, when I want the whole world to go to shit.

I know then that the moment has arrived for me to find a patio, order a beer, and pull out my Paper Mate 0.5 black.

85

HOW THE WEST WAS WON

In the year the Sun King moved definitively to Versailles, Philippe Rivages crossed France, boarded a merchant ship, sailed up the St. Lawrence and settled down in the area around Quebec City. While the former strolled in his gardens, snuffing tobacco around the fountains, the latter took the harder path of drawing life from the earth and conquering winter.

Three centuries later, Johnny Weissmuller made his last appearance on the big screen in *Won Ton Ton: The Dog Who Saved Hollywood*. It also turned out to be Rin Tin Tin's final role.

86

STATEMENT OF INTENT

On August 22, 2004, the Arte channel broadcast a Tarzan special. They screened two films and a documentary called *The One, the Only, the Real Tarzan*. It was the documentary that caught my attention. What really struck me was learning that the man who'd won five Olympic gold medals and broken twenty-eight world records in swimming, that this man, this legend, this myth, had ended his career as an actor in bad TV commercials, as a public amusement on talk shows, with a monkey on his knees. Worst of all, at the very end he was a host at a Las Vegas restaurant.

What was strangely disturbing during the whole documentary was that his famous smile never quit. I'm sure he must have died with a smile on his face.

Bad luck and the fall of icons fascinate me. The very moment of buckling, the way that glories can be erased, and how all lessons must be learned again. The emperor suddenly has no clothes. Maybe my fascination for Melville and Brautigan also stems from there. Two authors who scaled summits and who finished off much further down, the former forgotten, the latter with a bullet in his head. Paradise lost incarnated in men, irremediably.

That's why I wanted to recount the life of a man who came from nowhere. A child of Hungarian immigrants from the ghettos of Chicago, who had but one desire: to swim in Lake Michigan with his brother. He drops out of school. At twelve, he's an elevator boy. The future looks cloudy. His alcoholic father disappeared, his mother works at a restaurant.

One day, he's taken to a swimming club – that's his turning point. Upon seeing him, the coach knows he's witnessing the beginnings of an exceptional being, a future champion in the making. Soon after he makes his debut in athletic history, and then history all itself, when he becomes the first swimmer to finish the 100 meter in under a minute.

Beijing 2008, 100 meter freestyle, Alain Bernard: 47.21 seconds.

There are Olympic gold medals in Paris and Amsterdam. Then he leaves amateur swimming to become a spokesperson for a bathing suit company. He does events, lives at a hotel, grows rich.

By the same token that a swimmer was discovered at the age of sixteen, at thirty-two the Tarzan actor was discovered, making him a Hollywood star alongside the likes of Sinatra, Wayne, and Gable. It's the second apotheosis. They called him the worst actor in Hollywood. No one asked him to act, rather he was asked to swim, to sit on an elephant and carry a monkey on his shoulders.

The years passed and the boyish Adonis aged, gained weight, greyed. Around this time his accountant runs off with his cash. Johnny is ruined, broke. He attempts a comeback with Jungle Jim, but it doesn't lead to anything beyond that mediocre and shortlived TV series. There's nothing left of the glamor and the glitz, the Lupe Vélez years of the 1930s.

He'll get swindled again, by another accountant, and get divorced for a fourth time. His daughter Heidi dies in a car accident. His children file several lawsuits against him. After his first heart attack, he begins to lose his mind. It appears that during his stay at a recovery home, he began to think he really was Tarzan, and he belted out his famous cry at all hours of the day and night.

There you go, I wanted to cast a light on this exceptional athlete who pretty much got taken to the cleaners, who flew so high he came tumbling down like Icarus. He messed up his final plunge and finished off his days in Acapulco, kidnapped by his last wife, a fake baroness of sorts named Maria Brock Mandell Bauman who wanted to separate him from his family at all costs. In the biography of his father, Johnny Junior calls her the Black Widow.

He was born János. Upon arriving in America, he became Johnny. To convince others he was American, he took on the name of his brother Peter. He became Tarzan. When he died, Weissmuller was buried in the Valley of the Light cemetery. A few years ago, it was renamed. Johnny's remains now rest in the Gardens of Time.

87

A DIFFICULT MOMENT

In early January, I traveled down to Acapulco with my wife to visit my father. He was in a very dire state. He was delirious. He had trouble speaking. He wanted me to take him back to Hollywood so he could go party with his friends. I said to him, "Dad, all your friends are already gone. They're dead. No one's left but you. You're the last." He couldn't bring himself to believe me. He didn't want to believe it.

So there I was, sitting in front of an extremely weak man who was once the most well-known athlete of his time, the richest actor in Hollywood. He wore diapers now, he had a hole in his throat to facilitate his breathing, and a tube in his stomach for feeding. He was strapped down to the bed and could no longer move.

All he could do was look me right in the eyes and cry. It was a difficult moment to endure.

88

January 20, 1984. We're just learning of the death of Johnny Weissmuller at the age of seventy-nine. The five-time Olympic medalist and celebrity actor behind Tarzan the Ape Man has died following a battle with pulmonary edema. The athlete took his final breath at his home in Acapulco, where as an actor he had performed his final role. In the years since then, he'd retired there with his fifth wife.

Luis Flores, director of the Gomez funeral home, stated that Mr. Weissmuller's widow has yet to finalize funeral preparations, but that the burial would most likely take place Sunday in Acapulco. According to several sources, Weissmuller's children, who've been estranged from him and his last wife, would rather the body of their father return to Hollywood for a ceremony worthy of the fallen icon.

Weissmuller had been gravely ill for several years. He was the victim of numerous cardiac arrests. His Acapulco residence was situated next to the lake where he filmed his last Tarzan film. The home was all that remained from the real estate investments he'd made in the fifties alongside other actors—Sinatra, Bogart, and Wayne—who made Acapulco's beaches famous.

JOHNNY WEISSMULLER
1904 – 1984
R.I.P.

89

THE CRY

When military veterans or important statesmen are buried, a round of artillery is fired off, either by cannon or rifle. When Johnny Weissmuller's casket was lowered into the ground, as the cemetery employees steadily released the cables so the coffin could slide to the bottom of the hole, at that moment in the Acapulco cemetery, under a blazing sun, they played back Tarzan's cry. Three times over, the recording of that mythic cry pierced the mourners' silence. According to a witness, the effect was pathetic. The cry, full of vigor and power played at the very moment when Weissmuller's vanquished and defeated corpse touched its final resting place, the cry froze the blood of the too few people in attendance. We will never know if it was, indeed, his final wish.

90

POST-SCRIPTUM
IN MEMORY OF RICHARD BRAUTIGAN

I never learned how to make mayonnaise.

ESPLANADE
Books

THE FICTION SERIES AT VÉHICULE PRESS

A House by the Sea : A novel by Sikeena Karmali

A Short Journey by Car : Stories by Liam Durcan

Seventeen Tomatoes : Tales from Kashmir : Stories by Jaspreet Singh

Garbage Head : A novel by Christopher Willard

The Rent Collector : A novel by B. Glen Rotchin

Dead Man's Float : A novel by Nicholas Maes

Optique : Stories by Clayton Bailey

Out of Cleveland : Stories by Lolette Kuby

Pardon Our Monsters : Stories by Andrew Hood

Chef : A novel by Jaspreet Singh

Orfeo : A novel by Hans-Jürgen Greif
[Translated by Fred A. Reed]

Anna's Shadow : A novel by David Manicom

Sundre : A novel by Christopher Willard

Animals : A novel by Don LePan

Writing Personals : A novel by Lolette Kuby

Niko : A novel by Dimitri Nasrallah

Stopping for Strangers : Stories by Daniel Griffin

The Love Monster: A novel by Missy Marston

A Message for the Emperor : A novel by Mark Frutkin

New Tab : A novel by Guillaume Morissette

Swing in the House : Stories by Anita Anand

Breathing Lessons : A novel by Andy Sinclair

Ex-Yu : Stories by Josip Novakovich

The Goddess of Fireflies : A novel by Geneviève Pettersen
[Translated by Neil Smith]

All That Sang : A novella by Lydia Perović

Véhicule Press